Moss

Moss

Klaus Modick

TRANSLATED BY
David Herman

BELLEVUE LITERARY PRESS
New York, NY

First published in the United States in 2020
by Bellevue Literary Press, New York

For information, contact:
Bellevue Literary Press
www.blpress.org

Moss was originally published in German in 1984
as *Moos* by Haffmans Verlag.
Text © 1984 by Klaus Modick
© Verlag Kiepenheuer & Witsch GmbH & Co. KG,
Cologne, Germany
Translation © 2020 by David Herman

Library of Congress Cataloging-in-Publication Data
Names: Modick, Klaus, author. | Herman, David, 1962- translator.
Title: Moss / by Klaus Modick ; translated by David Herman.
Other titles: Moos. English
Description: First edition. | New York, NY : Bellevue Literary Press, 2020. |
    Moss was originally published in German in 1984 as Moos by Haffmans Verlag. |
    Translated from the German
Identifiers: LCCN 2019031919 (print) | LCCN 2019031920 (ebook) |
    ISBN 9781942658726 (trade paperback) | ISBN 9781942658733 (ebook)
Classification: LCC PT2673.O24 M613 2020 (print) | LCC PT2673.O24 (ebook)
    | DDC 833/.92--dc23
LC record available at https://lccn.loc.gov/2019031919
LC ebook record available at https://lccn.loc.gov/2019031920

Bellevue Literary Press would like to thank all its generous donors—individuals and foundations—for their support.

 This publication is made possible by the New York State Council on the Arts with the support of Governor Andrew M. Cuomo and the New York State Legislature.

 The translation of this work was supported by a grant from the Goethe-Institut.

Book design and composition by Mulberry Tree Press, Inc.

Bellevue Literary Press is committed to ecological stewardship in our book production practices, working to reduce our impact on the natural environment.

∞ This book is printed on acid-free paper.

Manufactured in the United States of America
First Edition

1 3 5 7 9 8 6 4 2

paperback ISBN: 978-1-942658-72-6

ebook ISBN: 978-1-942658-73-3

For M. J. G.

Moss

Preliminary Note
by the Editor

THE DEATH OF Professor Lukas Ohlburg, who died in the spring of 1981, at the age of seventy-three, has resonated far beyond the realm in which he did his botanical research, giving rise to expressions of sympathy and grief in the wider sphere of scientific life. Numerous obituaries and appreciations in newpapers and journals—and not just scientific journals—have noted that because of Ohlburg's death the natural sciences in general, as well as botany in particular, have sustained a considerable loss. Apart from his field-specific investigations, of which his two major studies of tropical and subtropical forms of vegetation have long been counted among the classics of modern botany, Ohlburg's essays critiquing the terminology of natural science have had a profound influence on theories about science itself. This work brought him not only significant acclaim but also strong criticism, given the nature of the subject and Ohlburg's deliberately provocative way of treating it.

In the narrow circle of Ohlburg's colleagues and friends, it was known that in the last years of his life he spoke frequently of wanting to combine these essays into a systematic work, which would bear the title *Toward a Critique of Botanical Terminology and Nomenclature*. It appeared, however, that he had never actually attacked this project; or at least no records or materials relating to it could be found in his unpublished scientific papers. I am honored that, in my capacity as Ohlburg's long-standing assistant, it fell to me to undertake the task of sifting through these papers and editing them as necessary—a task that has since been completed (see Lukas Ohlburg, *Botanical Reflections from the Unpublished Papers*, Munich, 1982). That volume could not have been assembled without the kind cooperation of the brother of the deceased, Professor Franz B. Ohlburg, of Hanover, and after its publication I received a letter from him, at the end of 1982. I reproduce here, with his generous permission, an abridged version of Prof. Ohlburg's letter, since it is of great importance for understanding the text published in what follows:

> *. . . You will receive a registered parcel by the same post; it contains a bundle of manuscript pages authored by my deceased brother. As you know, he left,*

along with the scientific texts that you edited, an even greater number of personal notes. These were, basically, diaries, which in accordance with his last will and testament I have destroyed unread. But as for the manuscript in question, for a long time I was uncertain whether it should be viewed as personal in nature or, rather, as a text suitable for publication. After repeated readings—made all the more difficult by the manuscript's having been written, in part, in shorthand—I have come to the conclusion that my brother did think of these materials as part of his planned Critique of Botanical Terminology and Nomenclature. *Publishing these materials may thus correspond to my brother's intentions, even though I have serious misgivings about taking that step. Before I express my concerns more fully, however, I need to communicate to you some of the details of my brother's death, because these details throw a peculiar light on a manuscript that is itself quite strange.*

My brother was, as officially announced, found dead in the country house in Ammerland that belonged to both of us. The date of his death, so far as that can be firmly established, was 3 May 1981; heart failure was given as the cause of death. My brother had secluded himself in this house starting in September 1980, in order to work on his project there. Although he was not in the best of health because of his heart disease, he insisted on taking care of himself, categorically refusing any help in the house. You probably know better than I how stubborn he could be, especially when he was working.

I visited him there at Christmas that year. He struck me as being happy, relaxed, and unusually upbeat. The only change I noticed was that he had let his beard grow out. His mental state appeared to be clear—though, looking back, I would now freely admit that some of his comments should have made me suspicious. On 11 May 1981, I received a phone call from the village police station, informing me that my brother had died. I drove there the same day. The farmer living in the neighborhood, Hennting, had alerted the police after my brother had failed to make his customary trip to the farm to pick up his mail and purchase any necessities.

When I first arrived in the house, my brother's corpse had already been taken to the village of Wiefelstede. The village doctor, who had issued the death certificate, gave me the following account: Despite the rainy weather of the preceding days, the doors and windows of the house had been left open. My brother was lying in front of his writing table, his body already slightly decomposed; the state of his body was attributable to the high moisture level in the house. Curiously, mossy growths were found on his face, particularly around his mouth, nose, and eyes, as well as in his beard. For understandable reasons, his corpse had to be put in a coffin immediately. But even so, with the exception of his overgrown beard, my brother's body did not strike me as being unkempt; nor did he appear to be undernourished. Similarly, the house was, as I made sure, in a clean and orderly condition, though with an odd exception: Patches and cushions of moss were scattered everywhere; the writing desk and likewise the floor were littered with them. Even the bed pillow was strewn with various mosses; some of these had withered, but others, because of the dampness in the house, were still green. This state of affairs explained the "mossification" of my brother's mortal remains. On his writing table lay, amid the mosses, the aforementioned manuscript as well as an uncapped fountain pen. Hence my brother seemed literally to have died at his desk.

Once you have read it, you will understand why I hesitated so long before releasing this text. Even as a lay botanist, I venture to say that that these pages are likely to be of little interest vis-à-vis botanical research. Indeed, I doubt that my brother wrote this text in full possession of his mental faculties. If, as his brother, I find the confusion of his thought and language regrettable, as a psychologist I find it alarming. Indeed, although my brother continually refers to the project as a critique of terminology, the text as a whole strikes me as being the psychogram of his advancing senility. Given that my brother's scientific reputation has never been subject to the slightest doubt, however, I will not block the publication of this text. Nevertheless, I do wish to express, in emphatic terms, my reservations concerning the views expressed herein. The title page, along with a few other passages, indicate that my brother wanted to publish the text. I believe that I am honoring his wishes in leaving this manuscript with you. . . .

So much for the statement of Dr. Franz B. Ohlburg, whose reservations I share. The manuscript itself arrived in a brown cardboard folder, its deep grooves probably caused by exposure to moisture. The chronological sequence in which the individual pages were composed cannot be reconstructed. In any case, Ohlburg must have continued to work on the project until just before his death, albeit sporadically. Having been written on normal typewriter paper, the manuscript is divided, ostensibly at least, into two parts. The first third is written in shorthand with a pencil, that being Ohlburg's preferred method of working. (He would later dictate his notes to his secretary.) But the last and greater part of the manuscript is written with a fountain pen in normal longhand, for which Ohlburg used green ink. The text itself goes into this matter. On the cardboard folder he used pencil to write the original title—*Toward a Critique of Botanical Terminology and Nomenclature*—in shorthand. Subsequently, though, this title was struck through with green ink and carefully rewritten as *Moss*. The prefatory quotation appears to have been copied down during this later phase, as well.

—K. M.
Hamburg, October 1983

Moss

And to the end I saw myself receding softly,
like smoke, into the pores of the earth.

—Annette von Droste-Hülshoff,
"In the Moss"

I SHOULD HAVE RETURNED here earlier. Did I dread the memory? I wanted to be productive, to push something forward, drive it out of myself—something whose meaning, however, seems more and more elusive to me, the longer and more passively I accept, in myself, a mere being here. This acceptance is equivalent to a serenity, a kind of farewell to the empirical world, which I am losing interest in, becoming indifferent to. Such indifference takes the form of nothing being more important to me than anything else.

At this point I barely read the newspapers, and I do not keep a television or radio near me, nor pay them any mind. For days I have felt a kind of dizziness, a fading away. This is not the feeling brought on by the brutal blows of my heart attack, which forced me to become an emeritus professor a few years ago. It is, rather, a feeling of being pulled softly downward, although the direction in question cannot be correctly described as downward. In general, since my arrival here my thoughts, ideas, and sensations are of directionlessness and aimlessness, difficult to define, gleaming in a faint clarity wholly unknown to me up to this point, a vague, indeterminate everywhere. The perception of this deconcentration, inimical to thought, is intense—indeed, overly clear. Although I did not come here to let myself go, I do not resist.

When we were children, there could be no talk of such instability, such groundlessness, because Father, even while on holiday here in the country, placed by far the greatest value on discipline—and by that he meant composure. Was that why, later on, I was never at ease in the house? It was only Franz and his family who spent summers here; I always traveled farther. Even now I find traces of my nephew, Franz's son, and his family in the house: children's drawings on the walls, a turntable with a collection of rock-music records, and textbooks on sociology and economics, most of them written from a neo-Marxian perspective.

Sometimes I enjoy browsing through these textbooks. I amuse myself by considering how they derive ridiculous problems from the most banal platitudes of a crude, primitive epistemology. They use a discourse that no longer even grasps its own content, because its concepts have choked out all intuition, because the abstract is too seldom brought into relation with the concrete; by way of compensation, the discourse inclines toward verbal tricks of an almost artistic sort. But through this very romanticization of scientific discourse, something like knowledge occasionally shines through.

Analytic and dialectical thinking has probably never led to understanding, to real knowledge, to truth in a comprehensive, almost metaphysical sense. As is well known, Hegel in his *Logic* poses the remarkably nonsensical question of whether it is not an "infinitely higher achievement to capture the form of the syllogism than to describe a species of parrot or a veronica plant"; and how much higher is such an achievement as compared to describing a humble moss! To be sure, contemporary science seeks to wash itself clean of such ignorantly arrogant rationalism; yet it washes and washes and still is not able to remove the stain of such nature-despising cynicism from its pale skin. If I only knew how to describe what a lower animal, a tree, or even a moss really is, I could care less about the 2,048 possible forms of logical syllogism that Leibniz enumerated in his combinatory analysis. He must have been very bored, that old couch potato. . . .

As for the botanical terminology used as a naming system for the natural phenomena in which, for example, this house lies embedded: In the best case it says only *what* grows here, albeit in a soulless and uncomprehending way. Never can it say *how*, and never with full certainty could it say *why*. And perhaps it is better that way.

When it comes to the magnificent old pine tree whose branches beat against my upper windows, I can name it "correctly" and conceptually disassemble it right down to its molecular structure. But I have no way of describing the language with which the tree, in knocking against the window, speaks to me.

UNDOUBTEDLY, BOTANY, like any science, requires a simple, clear, internationally accepted nomenclatural system. On the one hand, the terms of this nomenclature are used to mark off the various ranks within a taxonomy of systematically arranged groups or units; on the other hand, they function as scientific names that designate particular taxa of plant groups. But in my view it is undeniable that this very nomenclature, instead of deepening our knowledge of the objects and phenomena that it serves to classify, contributes to an always increasing estrangement of the researching subject from what he or she is investigating. The term, the name, does not simply provide a means for classifying a phenomenon or object; what is more, in being identified with or reduced to any such classification, the object or phenomenon is short-circuited, regarded as understood, as known.

Now to some degree, this way of proceeding is necessary in order for any general scientific consensus to be achieved; but it may be, in the final analysis, the goal of all science. What we find in contemporary botanical literature and research is a theory that yields classifications without real knowledge. I myself participated in this kind of research all my life, to the best of my ability and in good conscience—and with a not inconsiderable amount of success. I feel compelled, however, to think otherwise, to speak otherwise, before it is too late for me.

But how? In attempting to develop a plausible critique of botanical terminology, of scientific discourse in general, and ultimately of scientific thinking and method per se, I am faced with a dilemma. Is there a language that can capture and transmit real knowledge? (It remains to be clarified what this knowledge is—if it can, in fact, be "clarified.") Such a language must surely be one that renounces intersubjectively binding, one-dimensional cataloging and categorization; a language—and here is the paradox—that defines insofar as it gives expression to the undefinable. It must be a language that does justice to singularity and particularity, placing more trust in intuitions than fixed concepts.

As I write this down, I realize that in advancing such a construal of formal, academic science, I am getting lost, going astray. Among the circle of my highly esteemed colleagues, no one will take me seriously. Here I allow myself a way of thinking, a form of expression, that before I always warned my pupils, research students, and colleagues against. Yet it seems to me as though I were being allowed to use just this sort of language. But by whom?

A PICTURE-BOOK INDIAN SUMMER brings warm temperatures once again. At night one already gets an indistinct sense of fall, but by day it is still as warm as high summer. I take advantage of the weather by going swimming regularly. Toward evening, as the day gradually cools down, there is an exact instant when the water and air temperatures equalize. That is the best moment. No further transitions can be sensed; the specific qualities of the different states of matter melt into one another.

My physician has gently warned me to cut back on my swimming somewhat, but the half hour that I need to swim across the lake and back causes me no difficulty whatsoever. The slight tiredness that, without inducing sleepiness, comes over me more and more frequently, settling into my muscles and bones, dissipates when I swim. The weightlessness that water provides loosens

my muscles, eases my joints, and also sometimes drifts through my thoughts like a rising mist. For many people, walking relaxes
the mind; for me, it has always been swimming. The flow of my thoughts synchro-
nizes with the movements of my body. One
reaches far out and then, as it were, returns
back to oneself again. Taking swift breast-
strokes, I have sometimes planned out pre-
sentations, sometimes whole lectures.

Admittedly, it is no longer ideal for me
to swim that rapidly. As my physician has
said, shaking his forefinger at me in mock-
threatening fashion, just because we all
came from the water in the beginning is no
reason for me to meet my end there, as well.
Or do I in my old age want to throw my lot
in with the algae once again? Hence, swimming at a very leisurely pace, I pursue my
solitary tracks through the lake, which even
at high noon never looks blue, but, rather,

always shimmers with a green hue. Its color derives from the trees that line the lake and are, in turn, mirrored in it, but even more from the ever-increasing mossiness of the sandy shoreline.

There, as children, we hunted tadpoles, frogs, dragonflies, and the like. When I sit in the marsh grass on the embankment, which used to come up to my shoulders but now only reaches my waist, memories of these wanderings—and of the limitless adventures they brought—come vividly back to me. At the time we sought out not only ever new, as-yet-unknown shores of the lake but also this small, confined shoreline that, with its embankments and steep pits, held innumerable self-contained worlds, strange planets, deserts, jungles, wide savannas. After wandering here for hours, which were for us days, weeks, and years, we reappeared, overheated, red-faced, and confused by the reality of the family dinner table.

There must be some deep-seated drive to repeat the life course—not in an aging, senile regression, but productively, in the form of a readiness to bring the experiences of childhood back to life again. But what are remembered experiences? What are stories? The drive to repeat seems to become stronger the more one feels one's life slipping away. A circle completes itself. Beginnings come to an end. Knowledge terminates in experience, experience in memory, memory in narrated histories. The moss in which I take a rest from my swimming, and which oozes out through the gaps between my toes, assuming at this time of day the same temperature as the water and air, and the same temperature as my own body—the moss must be familiar with such processes, but also with the sense of futility that shadows this impulse to repeat, to relive the past.

Moss is certainly an archaic plant. Seemingly self-sufficient and at rest, for ages it has exhausted itself in what I would call a heroic struggle to adapt to life on dry land; and now, ossified in its initial design, it is clearly no longer capable of carrying to the end the evolutionary process that was once set into play within it. If plants have a capacity for memory, not a conscious or mental memory, but, rather, a genetic one—and I have no doubt that they do—the memory of mosses would be the memory of their emergence, their descent from algae. Moss cannot completely sever all ties with its own seagoing past. Hence the evolution of algae into moss has completed a pseudocycle, returning, albeit modified and at a higher qualitative level, to its starting point.

When I turn around and swim back to

the other shore, smiling at my physician's algae joke, I pause briefly in the middle of the lake to play the role of "dead man." I take a deep breath, lie motionless in the water, and squint at the setting sun, which hangs as if impaled on the tips of the pine trees. I ask myself whether there is any difference between sinking and rising, between the development of roots and the evolution of wings, between knowledge and wonder, between being and consciousness. I find no answers precisely because I am looking. I exhale deeply, slowly furthering my tracks through the lake.

As far as the working method that I use for my publications is concerned, it is my habit to set out in shorthand, from all the material collected in the first notes and drafts, what seems to be connected in principle with my main theme, no matter how remotely. Like Leibniz, I hold analogy to be a key factor in scientific progress, and often the most unexpected insights have emerged from such analogical clues. In science, accidents can come to one's aid only if one dismisses as irrelevant no observation, no impression—no matter how fleeting—and instead registers everything. As I now sift through and sort my first notes and excerpts for my *Critique of Botanical Terminology*, I realize that this time my strictly private, subjective perceptions, far from needing to be separated out from the treatise, are, in fact, central to the subject of the work.

Normally, I remove any personal remarks with which I have allowed my notes to become overgrown during the preparation of the manuscript for dictation; or at the latest, they are eliminated during the dictation process itself. Sometimes one or another of these impressions may be used as a speculative footnote. But what I am putting on paper now certainly belongs to the *Critique*, since it seems to me necessary to reflect not only on the thing itself but also and even especially on my own reflections about this thing— reflections that, precisely because of their personal nature, already constitute a critique of terminology. Indeed, since arriving here, my tendency to record everything that has anything to do with the object of my inquiry, even if only incidentally, has asserted itself even more. I am unable to assess at present whether this way of proceeding will be conducive or detrimental to my project.

Even my first pages, which I wanted to excise on account of their entirely private, diarylike quality, will have to remain where they are, because in certain respects they already get at the heart of my subject. Yet these pages also highlight the problem of method; at issue is an expansion of one's focus to include second-order phenomena, or observations about acts of observing, where fixed points of reference can no longer be found. Before I get swallowed up completely in a defense of method, I want to use a banal example to demonstrate to what extent my topic must necessarily get away from me, sliding a priori past its apparent limits. To repeat myself, it is just this sliding past, this exceeding of boundaries, that in a peculiar manner constitutes the subject at hand.

If one states that the cushion mosses of the order Grimmiales in the family Grimmiaceae, for example, fall within both the genus *Grimmia* and the genus *Rhacomitrium*, one has handled the classifications wholly correctly. But straightaway the floodgates to incomprehensible boundlessness, which botanical nomenclature should be able to dam up, are opened when one moves beyond the classification of mosses to their phenology. It would be reasonable to describe the cushion mosses of this taxonomic order as small-growing and appearing in a densely branched or grass-shaped arrangement, and to say that the Polster cushion mosses often present with a gray covering of hair; this covering results from the so-called glass hair, or colorless bristles, which crown the tips of each of the leaflets. One could then move on to the seasonal transformations of this moss's appearance, to the peculiarities of its reproductive system, and so on and so forth. But such descriptions are already profoundly questionable and would be cast in different terms by different observers.

If one now states further that these mosses, when it comes to their preferred habitat, like to cover rocks, cliffs, walls, and old roofs with thick cushions, the stone that one has thrown into the water of reality, in using such concepts, stirs up even more waves. For it is not just that the appearance of the moss changes in accordance with changes in its habitat but that, conversely, the appearance of a given environment is altered through its being inhabited by moss. Thus observations based on sensory stimuli, which the observer receives by coming into tactile contact with the moss, fall completely outside the purview of every abstract conceptual scheme.

By the way, the most questionable phenomenon that remains to be discussed vis-à-vis this simple example involving the phenology of moss is its specific odor, which probably cannot be conceptually fixed at all. Generally speaking, the perception of smell is a phenomenon that throws into relief the phenomenalism of natural science; this emphasis on sensory stimuli as foundational is the reason why there is in science a strong theoretical consensus about terminology, but virtually no real knowledge. At least I myself have never heard any of my colleagues speak about (let alone give a lecture on) how the smell of moss may have awakened in him insights into its nature; and by the same token, no one talks about his relationship to moss, leaving aside other, more out-of-the-way things that have become associated with the moss's smell. This anesthetizing of the space of scientific knowledge, which science imposes on itself, was brought home to me in a very vivid way yesterday.

When my father had this house built around 1900, the roof was fully covered with thatch. Over the course of time, areas of the roof became damaged, and these were repaired, little by little, with red tile, early on for reasons of cost and later because one could scarcely find a thatch roofer able to make repairs. By the time of my arrival, I saw with great pleasure that gray cushion moss had almost completely covered over the sections of tile interspersed with the original roofing, and that in its color and its natural structure the moss had connected up harmoniously with the thatch.

In the house, I discovered a note from my brother, in which he told me what to watch out for in using the house, where one turns on the water and the electricity, and other information of this sort. Because I have not lived in the house since my childhood, these tips were useful and necessary. My brother's note ended with the announcement that in the next few days tradesmen that he had hired would come to the house to clean the moss off the roof tiles. This would be a favorable opportunity for the cleaning, given that I would now be living on-site for a while and could oversee the carrying out of the work. In contrast with my brother, who in this respect probably takes strongly after my father, I tend toward a certain laissez-faire in practical matters. What is more, I am of the opinion that nature should be left to its own devices, that we should allow it to exist in a certain symbiosis with the circumstances and spaces of our lives, and that we should fight against it only if it becomes truly threatening. But where is the limit? In any case, I did not wish to quarrel with my brother about this matter; I attached no real importance to it.

All that changed in a quite painful way when the roofer appeared yesterday with his apprentice, took a look at the roof, and, in his taciturn manner, muttered in the broad Ammerland dialect something about the work's being superfluous. But if the master, my brother, believed it needed to be done, that would always be all right by him. The two of them started on the work right away;

as they did so, I set about arranging my notes at my writing desk. Above my head began the sound of scraping, brushing, and scratching, far away and quietly at first, without really disturbing me. But the longer it went on, the more jarringly and intrusively the sounds penetrated through the ceiling, as though they were aimed right at me. There are certain inconspicuous sounds that, once we notice them and begin to wait for them, take on the moment they arrive unusually disruptive, disproportionate dimensions. The best example is a dripping water faucet, whose *tock, tock, tock* can swell explosively if one spends sleepless nights listening, with bated breath, for its rhythm.

It may be that a nervous irritability that always sets in when I begin a project made the whole situation more intense; but in any event, the noise from above grew so violent and threatening that I stood up from my writing table and, covering my ears, paced back and forth in the room. The more I tried to push the sound away, to evade it, the more mercilessly it bore down into my head, setting into motion vibrating oscillations that began to radiate throughout my entire body. I tried to concentrate, tried to distract myself with clear, logical thinking. In vain. I broke out in a sweat, and began to tremble in fear of a heart attack. In my agitation, I passed my hand again and again through my hair, as the scratching above seemed to take on the sound of a metallic rattle.

Out of the pit of my stomach a feeling rose upward, reaching my throat; but before the tears could well up in my eyes, the memory returned of another flood of tears—tears I had cried when my father lured me to visit a barber just before my first day of school. I had not known what awaited me there; but as the rattle of the scissors gets closer to my ears, I am invaded by an uncontrolled fear. This fear is behind my impotent attempt to melt, under the nimble hands of the barber, into an endless stream of tears in order to save my streaming hair. Through my deafening howl penetrates the well-intentioned but brutal laugh of the barber and the stern voice of my father: "Don't be a little girl!"

Later, my mother takes care that my tears have all dried; but as she brushes her hand through my hair, through these sparse remains, there is in her touch a wordless sadness, which is only slightly mitigated by her effort to console me.

I had stopped running my hand through my hair, because now the noise of the work being done on the roof sounded normal again. There was nothing there other than two roofers, scraping away the moss. I went outside to offer them both a cup of tea. By the time the sugar cube dissolved under the hot stream of tea, I had fully returned to myself. Would it bother them to leave off the work now, half-finished though it might be? I had realized that the moss, as a rootless, wood-free plant, could in no way damage the tiles. The head roofer stared at me in surprise.

"First one way, then another. City slickers!"

I insisted on paying him immediately, and gave him such an extraordinarily generous tip that the well-meaning incomprehension in the man's eyes almost turned into distrust.

"You would know best, Professor."

Shaking his head, he packed up his work tools and ladders. The apprentice wanted to sweep up the patches of moss that had fallen from the roof to the ground. I forbade him. When the engine noise of the roofers' van was swallowed up by the trees protecting the house, I felt better.

Could the correspondence between me

and the moss on the roof that this incident created, or rather brought to the surface, be summarized in the botanist's terse language? Perhaps in this manner: Although they are wood-free and rootless, mosses have an astounding ability to survive dry conditions during long periods of drought, only to revive again unexpectedly when new moisture arrives. A banal example—something that every first-year student learns. But we come to know something only if we have witnessed it, or perhaps only if we have lived it.

Was this what I wanted to say? I am no longer certain.

I AM WRITING DOWN THESE NOTES in fits and starts, in stark contrast with my usual habits. But the notes are dictated by no deadline; no audience, no publication, is awaiting their completion. And as the subject, the problem, becomes unclear to me via detached observation, where systematically controlled constraints emerge from a process of analysis; as the subject takes on dimensions the mere idea of which would have seemed unthinkable a short time ago, growing out past its former boundaries like a moss in the rain—as this process evolves, it seems to me as though I am not writing, but, rather, allowing the writing to happen. Or, more precisely, it seems as though I am allowing something other than me to write in and through me.

This feeling, which amounts to a huge sense of relief, the relief of being delivered from all responsibility, came over me one morning. In a manner that was again contrary to my usual modus operandi, I started working on the manuscript even before breakfast, right after I woke up, almost during the waking process itself. The doubts of a fully awakened, scientific consciousness were still dimly cocooned in the reality of dreams, and while I used my pencil to write in shorthand, there lay in the movement of the hand, in the metallic scratching down of abstract signs, a memory reaching back to far earlier times. As though it had been archived in the muscles of my hand and the hectic nervousness of the stenographic script, a warm electrical current crept out of my memory into the breaking dawn.

Year after year, the first day of our family holiday at the country house was dedicated to the same rituals. As soon as old Henschel had picked us up in the hackney carriage—as soon as the bags had been brought in through the entrance and Henschel made the drive back to Oldenburg with tip in hand—Mother went into the house with a local girl, whose name I strangely cannot remember (only her lavish reddish blond hair), to "clear the decks," as my father used to call all cleaning work. He himself immediately began his "start-of-the-visit route," which led from the Hennting farm past the forester's place in Dringenburg and ended up at the tavern in Spohle. There, along with teachers and the local minister, he drank a toast—via small beers and schnapps—to the headmaster's being once more on holiday with his family.

And while my father swam along on the alcohol-saturated joys of country life, while Mother and the girl slathered the entire house with enormous amounts of Pine-Sol, my brother and I did what my father had declared to be our duty. The path leading up to and around the house, as well as the uncovered terrace on the south side, were then, just like today, paved with brown-red bricks, which had been baked in the Nethen brickworks. During the springtime rains, grasses, herbs, and mosses established themselves in the narrow joints of sand between the individual bricks; and where the rain spilled out from the gutters on the roof, these plants had already begun tentatively to grow over the joints and lay their green luster on top of the earthy red of the bricks. Every year upon our arrival at the house, my father used to rest his hands on his hips and to call out in mock outrage, "What is all this? The green stuff is getting thick again. Get after it! The wild growth must be stopped! Duty calls!"

And he would press into Franz's hand as well as my own a wire brush, mumble something along the lines of "completely" or "root and branch," and take his leave, whistling as he marched off in the direction of the tavern in Spohle. Out of the house came the sounds of the women's scouring and wiping as we got down on our knees and used the wire brushes to cut the grassy heads of hair and rip to pieces the pillows of moss.

Once I had objected: "But the moss is so lovely."

"Lovely?" My father had shaken his head indulgently. "What is harmful, my child, what is harmful is never lovely. Everything in its proper time. Everything in its proper place. There"—as he gestured toward the woods—"there is the moss. And here"—as he pointed to the brick—"here we are. Everything must be in order."

My father was considered to be an excellent pedagogue. Hence we, his sons, scratched at the moss until our hands burned and our backs and knees ached, so that our father upon his return could say, from out of a hazy fog of schnapps and beer, what he always said: "You see? Here one can really live."

When I lay in bed, when the room was flooded by night and dreams—not the gray night of the city, but, rather, the blue-and-green night that came in through window, roof, and walls—I felt every single muscle in my hand, which had guided the wire brush. I felt the pain diminish in the pulsing of my blood, although I did not know whether the pain was mine or that of the moss. I heard the harsh scraping of the wire finger, the wire hand, on the dry bricks, fell asleep in the endless back-and-forth of my hand, which moved over the brick, just as it scratched over slate tablets, drew up infinitely long love letters, signed a thousand documents, hastily used a pencil to arrest my thoughts in a leaden fixity, lacerated—but also described—the moss.

As I sit on the terrace in the warm September sun and write these lines in shorthand, I see that all the joints between the bricks are grown over with moss; the red surface is covered with a veil of green. I take off my shoes and walk barefoot over this veil. Always in a circle, always in a circle. The veil lifts, swirls around my hand. A wind blows tiredly from the south. Always in a circle. The great pine tree leans down toward me. I know it speaks, but I am deaf. I go in a circle. The bricks are warm; the moss is cool. The bricks are dry; the moss is moist. Always in a circle.

"HERE ONE CAN REALLY LIVE," my father shouted out jovially when the wire brushes had won their annual struggle against the wild growth of the mosses. If he had known how well one can die here, too, if only the wild growth is allowed to take its natural course, he would perhaps have been spared a horrible half year in the hospital ward for hopeless cases. As we gathered around the sterile bed, the whole family was more relieved than saddened by his last words—"Now I don't understand anything anymore"—because his suffering was finally over. All this had only made his passing more difficult for him. Rather than being able to demonstrate his cheerful, loud strength, he floated off into a mute helplessness.

In the face of the big sleep, his lifelong slogan, "Reason delights," must have seemed to him the great error of his life. I watched him descend to a place where really there is nothing more to understand; and then I euthanized my own fear by engaging with Franz in all-night debates. We argued about which biological terms can most precisely delineate the death of living tissue. Franz reached eagerly after materialistic explanations that explain nothing, because he, with his psychology, was shoved up against the limits of the mind sooner than was I, with my biology. I had an arsenal of concepts that, by way of the symbolic language of chemical compounds, ultimately misconceives and masks the mystery of death as a scientifically knowable process. As for the panicky agitation that shot out from my father's eyes at that time, we kept that quietly under lock and key. Looking back, I realize that my father, who knew every bird, could assign every tree its Latin name, warded off with these terms his fear of nature, the disquiet that pounced on him when the moss swelled up out of the joints between the bricks. The terms were my father's intellectual wire brushes. And so have I—the beloved son, the good child—kept my father's fear alive for another lifetime. This fear has driven me to such heights of my profession that the peak I have reached is now finally beginning to crumble.

In essence the problem can be described thus: The artificial constructions of conceptual exactitude, which have given unique terms their internationally binding force—terms with which Linnaeus two hundred years ago made daisies *Bellis perennis*—have not given names to nature, but, rather, stolen names from it. In other respects as well, Linnaeus's nomenclature is a difficult inheritance, for its system is not merely descriptive but also strangely, and infamously, evaluative. It is simply outrageous that the chimpanzee is denigrated as *troglodytes*, the orangutan as *satyrus*. And it is a feeble joke for Linnaeus to have given the amoebas the name *Chaos chaos*. After all, amoebas are the atoms of biological and therefore also logical order. The label *Chaos chaos* can with equal, if not greater, justice be applied to Linnaeus's own nomenclature!

The annihilation of the name through the concept, of the living expression through the scientific term, has sped up and sealed humankind's alienation from the surrounding natural world. In the natural course of things, the complete loss of a name, of form, occurs only in death, in which beings decay and enter into a great formlessness, just as brooks, rivers, and streams lose their names when they flow into the sea. In the same way, when in the past prisoners were identified with numbers, they were stricken from the list of persons, and exiled to a space devoid of memory. Even when it comes to sites, places, and cities, this process of numbering does not stop; thus post codes are destroying our very homes. The use of numbers instead of names for streets in the United States always disturbed me during my years there. Now I know why.

I can hear my colleagues voice their doubts about whether I'm still in my right mind. In reply, I say that I have seldom felt as sane as I feel these days.

That plants, animals, persons, streets, and places have names is, in fact, only part of the truth about the relationships between words and reality. The other part, which slips past us, is that names themselves comprise things, that names *are* things, that around names fields of force have taken shape; by means of these force fields, the material and intellectual reality of the surrounding environment interpolates itself into a name. In this way, things bespeak their life. An established name is thus, biologically conceived, the result of a mimetic process.

We know about the protective adaptations of many animals; thanks above all to their color, but sometimes also their form, these creatures can match their appearance to the animate and inanimate bodies in their environment. Analogously, the mimetic properties of names seem to radiate out toward all that has been, toward all that is now living, and to reveal their full potential in the face of death. Living life: That is what a name preserves. Perhaps that is also the reason why this knowledge has only now, toward the end, penetrated through the tank armor of science to reach me. If adaptations of the sort that extend beyond us are achieved through the medium of names, it must be possible to use this medium not only to trace past experiences but also to map out future ones. In just the same way, all things human were anticipated long ago in the plant.

Strange thoughts on which I have come to dwell. Or have these thoughts, rather, come to dwell in me? In actuality, these are not thoughts, but, rather, experiences—experiences that the nature of this place has given to me and unlocked ever since I began no longer merely to visit but also to get involved with, or in, the place. Indeed, what made it clear to me that names radiate their mimetic force only through such interconnected experiences, to which rationalistic inquiry, however, remains closed, is the name of this place: Mollberg. In its minor key, its *Moll*, resonates the serene, melancholic, but not resigned musicality that is woven from the sounds of nature and pulsates audibly through the place. In strict geographic terms, Mollberg belongs to Dringenburg; but it is a sign of the local residents' indigenous sensitivity to place that they have always felt this whole area belonged with the name Mollberg. It is the area around the small lakes on whose shorelines the machinery of a onetime gravel mine gradually falls into weather-beaten disuse, becoming nature once again. Here are oak and pine forests, with fields that, offering wide vistas, are bordered by wildflowers; there are also dusty brick paths leading through bird-filled hedgerows. Yes, let geography be geography: It is truly a rare art to be able to let things be! Likewise, no matter how far and wide you look, throughout the whole of the Mollberg area there is no mountain, no *berg*. Some other kind of elevation must be at stake, then—an ascent of a mental sort, perhaps. In the end, I simply do not want to know.

The melancholy of the place that its name bespeaks—the melancholy of the inde-terminacy of its name, which appears to lie over the country like an unwritten history—is also the melancholy of the passage of time. Everything here is so unexciting and unos-tentatious that, barring the risk of finding a long stay burdensome, one always wants to remain. This remaining, this letting oneself be, is a temperate swim in a landscape that brings no cause for fear. It is simply there, lovely, mild, and very green. When it rains, the landscape becomes blue, as in certain Romantic paintings, and happily offers up its lush fertility for consideration. The only attraction here is that of having my thoughts soothed with memories that grow over me, soft as a moss, from all quarters.

These memories empty time of duration. Days lose their dates, thoughts their pompous urgency, their grimace of haste. When, as now, at the end of September, yellow blends with the lusty plumpness of summer, as it gently cools down; when birch leaves drop palely on the paths; when in the autumnal withering one last greenness shimmers, soon to be exhausted—it is then I know that a year holds everything, both taking and giving; that a year is nothing but a glance, a batting of the eyelashes, a casual intake of nature's breath. Mollberg is—I know no better words to use for it than the ones I once read—rediscovered time. As a child, I had time. It was endless then and did not matter. The present was always there. Then came life; time, at that point, possessed me. Now death approaches and time will be returned to me.

And how clearheaded I am!

Since my arrival here, I have not shaved. After I came to the house, I discovered that I had forgotten to bring my razor blades, but I did not want to make a special trip to Dringenburg just for that. When I went for my weekly shopping trip, I got myself some blades; the tough beard stubble began to be bothersome, rubbing on my shirt collars and causing my face to feel at once taut and ticklish. Yet when I finally sat with lathered face in front of the mirror and tried to shave the first tracks across my cheeks, my skin became so unbearably irritated that I stopped with a pain-distorted grimace.

At the place near my right ear where I had initiated my shaving attempt, I had inflicted upon myself a cut that was bleeding heavily. In addition, this shaved patch of skin immediately began to turn a dark red and was covered with rashlike pimples. Angrily, I wiped the shaving cream from my face, although the word *anger* does not capture the feeling that gripped me. A fearful uneasiness warned me that the old man in the mirror no longer had the steadiness of hand required to shave himself, that the beard, against which he would no longer be able to struggle single-handedly, would continue to sprout until the end, an outwardly visible sign of his decline. But this scornful self-knowledge, this insight into the helplessness of the old, became entangled with the thought that my body had, in effect, protested against an unnatural intervention into its growth; that the corporeal decline this protest had brought to the surface also began to bring forth in me a new quality, a wellspring emerging from my own desiccation.

I sat in front of the mirror and stared into the wasted stubble landscape of my face, from which the blood from the cut on my jawbone dripped slowly downward. I watched as the white-gray frill on my upper lip began to move in a blur, lost definition, changed color—becoming a blond fuzz on sun-browned skin, which, now that I'm again back in the bleak classroom after the summer holidays, will soon be bleached out. Into my reverie comes the roar of the North Sea surf, the rustle of the dune and beach grasses, the cries and bleating of the gulls, and from very far away a voice calling my name. Tziebäcke, my bench mate, pokes me in the side.

"Lukas!"

"Yes?"

"Having a good sleep, Ohlburg?" The mocking voice of senior teacher Dr. Wölk. "Would you please do us the favor of reciting the masterpiece of German poetry for which you were to prepare? If you please, *Mr.* Ohlburg!"

Tziebäcke shrugs his shoulders, smiling ruefully. Felmhofer grins mischievously; Eilert smirks. I rise from the bench and stand in the aisle between the seats. Through the open portion of the window, the part whose prospect is not clouded by milky glass, streams the holiday sun.

"Conrad Ferdinand Meyer. 'Afterglow in the Woods.'

'Into the forest I went . . .'"

"Fled," whispered Tziebäcke.

"Uh, 'fled, / A wild animal hunted to death.' Uh . . ."

Tziebäcke shrugs his shoulders again.

Wölk's mocking nasal voice: "Tomorrow you will know this. Perfectly. And with an appropriate emphasis, if you please. And add to it Meyer's 'Feet in the Fire.' But with the correct emphasis, Ohlburg. This is lyric poetry; this is magic. You ruin it all with your stammering. Ohlburg, man! What do you plan on doing with your life? Sit down! Obbie, recite this for us."

Obbie is at the top of the class. He recites the poem. But does Wölk take his oily singsong recitation to be an appropriate emphasis?

> Into the forest I fled,
> A wild animal hunted to death.
> There the last glow of the sun
> Streams down smooth tree trunks.

I drift back to Wangerooge Island, back to the sand, back to the sea, and through the wind comes the German poetry that Obbie is droning out.

> I lie panting. Behold, to my side
> The moss and stone are
>   bleeding—

There was more to it, something else. What was it?

> The blood streams out of my
> wounds
> Or is it the evening light?

The red clot of blood in the moss of my beard crusted over scabbily. I continued to stare at myself, saw a stranger, frightened of himself. Where was that? When is that? That skeptical look, that disgust at the growth of the beard?

Mother says, "Boy, look at yourself."

Traffic noise, flushing toilets, showers. Strange smells, a strange language, which was at one time familiar to me, very familiar. The tiny, dirty hotel room. Chelsea. London, at the beginning of 1934. The crossing was terrible, the ferry overcrowded, luggage in the corridors, vomit everywhere. I am seasick. I curse continuously.

Franz says over and over again, "Be glad that we're getting out."

Of course, he is so right, so terribly right. But I cannot, still do not want to believe it. Why were we all so sure of ourselves, Father, Mandelbaum, I? When Father was suspended from his position, father of all people, with all his good breeding and sense of order, we should have been warned. At the very latest. Or even earlier—namely, one year before, when Marjorie packed her bags and left.

"You folks are crazy," she kept saying at the train platform through her tears. "You folks are crazy. You call that science? You call that politics? I call it mysticism, plain mysticism."

It certainly was idiocy that flooded the universities at that time—race, blood, the whole absurd irrationalism, which poured out in an ever more brazen way from the lecterns. And as for us botanists, us biologists: Ironically, our fellow students abandoned their enthusiastic, intoxicated pursuit of knowledge; let the truth be the truth; preached nation, blood, and soil; forced Mandelbaum, who had spoken publicly about the death throes of such backward people, into retirement. He fled to the United States. At first, we laughed about it all, but it was a doubtful, desperate laughter. With Mandelbaum's exodus, our laughter died away.

Then came Father's dismissal, Father, who in front of his students had railed against the government as a pack of uncultured, ill-bred philistines on the chase, and then our pamphlet, in which we made fun of the so-called race theory and which we distributed in the institute. I was forced to ex-matriculate; Franz, shortly before graduation, was expelled from high school. One night, as Father drunkenly made his way home, he was beaten up. Mother's eyes were suddenly opened; she made up her mind. The house was sold. Our bags were packed, and the furniture followed later—to London. Franz and I came next. Bleary-eyed and dirty, we arrived.

"Boy, take a look at yourself. For God's sake! But the main thing is that you both are here."

I look in the mirror, disgusted with my five-day-old beard. So before I fall dead tired onto the bed, I shave myself, heavy-handedly, not concentrating, slashing myself. You have to fight it; you cannot just let it grow. It overgrows us, devours us. As I am falling asleep, I hear Franz say that he wants to study psychology, perhaps in Sweden, perhaps in the United States. He is already practicing it, saying, "Shaving oneself is the most subtle form of masochism."

He laughs; I sleep. I dream of algae,

brown algae, ferns, beards, mosses. It grows all over me.

I started, sitting before the mirror, and had the feeling that it was in a certain sense no accident that I had forgotten my razor blades. Forgetting helps us to remember. Now my beard has outgrown the stubble phase. It is soft. I have accepted it. I look in the mirror. I am glad that I am changing.

IF EVEN NAMES CAN BE MIMETIC, imitating things in the medium of sound, all the more can one shape imitate another in the medium of disinterested observation. When it comes to my devoting more and more attention to the carpet of moss on the terrace, Franz would no doubt explain this behavior via developmental psychology: I seem finally to have succeeded in disentangling myself from Father. It is not that simple, however;

it is even simpler. For when I touch the moss
with my feet, at the same time the moss
also touches my feet. The moss attracts me
even as I turn toward it. But the more firmly
I renounce an analytic, terminologically
driven, category-bound way of seeing, the
more I lose the botanist's penetrating gaze,
and the more powerfully I seem to attract the
moss. Do you understand what I am saying?

It is common knowledge that plants feel
a much stronger affinity to humans than to
other living beings. Experiments have even
shown that plants react especially violently
to the dying of the cells in the human body.
Of course, these experiments have always
been dismissed as charlatanism and mysticism by conventional science, and I myself
have, with my polemic against J. C. Bose's
Response in the Living and Non-Living, participated in this desperate attempt at so-called
objectivity, this effort to seal off the domain

of knowledge from the domain of experience. But here and now my old objections, disintegrating into the humus of experience, are wearing down. Surely there exists a realm in which something can transition from one point to another, from one organism into another, without time and space being relevant in any essential way.

I sense clearly that a form of communication between the moss and me is being established, that I am not only an observer but also subject to observation, even if I do not yet understand the language in which this communication is taking place. To be sure, it is not the language of which I am currently making use. And even if I were able to dissolve my categorizing habits of thought in the solution of some other kind of language, to make transparent that which does not clarify but, rather, amazes and astonishes, the communication would presumably be such that I could scarcely reflect on it in writing. And yet! As I alternate between squinting at the moss in which my feet rest, and then turning my gaze again to the paper that my hand covers with these signs, these images, there is a kind of resemblance.

I must explain this. But to whom?

For me, often, events that seem annoying or troublesome when they occur, or that are consigned to oblivion as irrelevant, sooner or later prove to be meaningful. These are the correspondences whose meaning is first revealed when suddenly, unbidden, they shoot into view, like a flash of lightning. In just this way, it seemed to me that by switching my glance from moss to paper, from paper to moss, some unpleasant truths were brought home to me once again. Ever since the memory of all that lethal scratching with the wire brush had come back to me via my recently adopted practice of morning stenography, it became acutely disgusting to me to continue to note down such details in shorthand. So I dug out my fountain pen, which, however, was all dried up. There was no ink to be found in the house. When I bicycled over to Spohle in the afternoon, on my usual shopping trip, I asked about ink at the supermarket into which Hansen's grocery store has mutated. They carried it, but because ink is apparently seldom needed there, only green ink was available.

"We are all out of blue," said the saleswoman. "Black, as well. Does that matter?"

Until at this moment, it did not matter to me; it had not mattered five minutes, or five hours, earlier. What's the difference? It's unimportant. But that I have found my way back to ink after all—ink, which does not scratch the paper, but, rather, slowly and softly sinks into it; that I have found my way back to handwriting—handwriting, which creates images in place of abstract steno-graphic symbols—all of this is, in truth, not unimportant.

Notice, for example, that the double *o* in the German word for moss, *Moos*, mirrors the shape of my spectacles. And just as I begin to take a sharper look at this, by not fixing my gaze exactly, there it is: the binocular microscope in the botanical institute. The place smells foul and a few of the students have gotten sick, even though the windows stand wide open. Yet the hot wind coming down from the Alps, under which Munich has groaned for the past three days, creeps inside. Our seminar is on tracking life, on chlorophyll, on greenery and verdure. Marjorie Garfield, the visiting student from Scotland, stands next to me and with her right eye investigates life through the microscope. Her left eye, however, penetrates my right eye, just as my right eye penetrates her left.

In turn, my left eye penetrates into the structure of the cells. We hear Professor Mandelbaum's voice, Mandelbaum, whom we, of course, call "the old man," Mandelbaum, who presents his inspiring analyses, or rather preaches them.

"And so on our planet, gentlemen— ladies and gentlemen . . ."

Marjorie blinks.

". . . living matter originates from plants, and only from plants! Therefore the totality of plants represents what ecological science designates as primary production, whose sole purpose is this: to be consumed by more complex living beings, animal as well human. The algae, the mosses, more generally all the ground plants that follow algae and mosses in their life histories, live on water, light, air, and minerals. In a synthesis of the material and the immaterial, the four elements of water, air, light, and earth merge in order to form, through this combination, the plants' living flesh. Ohlburg! You are not concentrating. Take a careful look; otherwise, you will see nothing."

Marjorie blinks. Her hair glows in the afternoon sun.

"A magical synthesis, which is reserved for plants alone, inaccessible to human science. And I say that, gentlemen—ladies and gentlemen—as both a scientist and a human."

Laughter around the microscopes.

"Garfield! You are not concentrating, either. In many primitive creatures, for example, in those you can observe directly, hence the whip algae, *Chlamydomonas* ... Ohlburg! Repeat the name!"

"*Chlamydo* ... uh ..."

"Take a better look! Everything lies right there within your view!"

Marjorie smiles.

"In primitive creatures, sexual union

obtains between two absolutely identitical cells, whose sex cannot be ascertained."

The sweat runs into my eyes. Marjorie has dark patches under her armpits.

"The powerful attraction, which suddenly draws one cell to another, may be the result of certain chemical secretions."

The patches under her armpits.

"Thus, the subtle dialectical play of attraction, on the one side, and retreat, on the other side . . ."

Marjorie coughs slightly.

". . . is already detectable in the most primitive life forms."

I wipe the sweat out of my eyes and remove the moisture from my glasses.

"A quarter past five, in the English garden," I whisper to Marjorie.

"Scottish revival," she whispers back.

"That should be enough, gentlemen—ladies and gentlemen," Mandelbaum says.

"Ohlburg!" he calls to me as we stroll out of the classroom. "Ohlburg! You should be more attentive. Next week we will investigate the mosses—but in great detail. So things will get even more complicated, my dear fellow. But"—and here he smiles at me—"there is also plenty of moss in the English garden. So study it well."

Study it well . . .

Ah, of course, the double *o*. Oh no, my finding my way back to handwriting is absolutely not a matter of indifference. And there being only green ink in Spohle is likewise anything but unimportant. We are indifferent only if we hold certain things to be more significant than others. But they are all equally valid.

The interests of our lives, and even more our deaths, are interwoven in manifold ways. So much so that happiness has often already been created and mapped out even while we still believe we are suffering.

THE WAY TO THE HENNTING FARM leads past the collapsed conveyor systems and sheds of a dilapidated gravel quarry. The farm is where I get my vegetables, eggs, and, for the past several weeks (to my own amazement), milk—milk, which I like and whose taste pleases me, even though I have reacted to it since my childhood with disgust and with physical allergies in the form of a red skin rash. During my previous few trips along this route at dusk, which arrives ever earlier, my attention was repeatedly drawn to a weak green-blue light, which appeared to stream out of a cavernous buried concrete silo.

The first time I encountered it, I took the flickering to be an irritation of my overtired eyes. I had spent, or, rather, squandered, the whole day reading Engler's *Syllabus of Plant Families*. When I removed my spectacles and rubbed my eyes, the light phenomenon vanished immediately. Although the following night I had dreams in which the light played a certain role, but which I could not remember the next morning, I soon forgot all about the incident. One week later, on the same route and at the same time of day but in a darkness that by then had already progressed further, I had the same perception; this time, however, it did not disappear when I removed my glasses. Yet as I took a couple of steps toward the silo, I lost sight of the apparition. I determined to get to the bottom of the matter the next evening.

It was almost pitch-dark when, stumbling over natural debris and scattered concrete rubble, I made my way through the entrance to the silo, which was overgrown with ivy and dense moss. As soon as I switched off my flashlight, light began to radiate from the walls and floor. It issued from particular points but was dispersed in a diffuse shimmer like weak, cloud-overcast moonlight. The botanical-analytic explanation is simple, for the so-called luminous or luminescent moss prefers to live in moist rocky crevices and cavities. It is difficult to find, being extremely small-growing and inconspicuous, but it reveals itself through a faint blue-green shimmering light, which comes about in the simplest possible way. The chlorophyll bodies in the moss absorb more light during the day than the plant needs in the way of energy. This surplus energy is then given off again, producing the shimmer that irritated but also attracted me.

I turned my flashlight back on in order to examine the moss up close, but as I touch the ground with my bent knee, suddenly it is an autumn afternoon here. Our bare knees press into the concrete floor of the half-built silo house—parents being held liable then for children's forbidden entry into this place. The moment has come where the promises of the chemistry kit must make the transition from trial to truth, experiment to event. We bend ourselves over the green mass of fluorescent phosphorus. Franz strikes the match; the jet of flame races over his arm and shoots into my eyes; we run to the exit, screaming as we emerge from the thick smoke into the brightness. But all is covered over with a milky veil. Later the sun comes back, because the glasses that I get are strong, with a small brass rim that pinches the wings of my nose. If I read too long, I get a headache. Now and then things flicker around me. I wipe my eyes and notice that the beam of the flashlight has become weaker.

Has the moss preserved my horror all these years—sixty years, it must be?

Preserved it undisturbed? Was I in this place so long? Going back sixty years? Or more? Or less? The luminous moss is a simply explained phenomenon. The excess energy is stored and later, much later, it radiates out of the plant. It is an optical echo, an echo of light, an echo image. A phenomenon that can be explained quite simply, this luminescent moss. But what does it know? What does it show? What is it communicating to me? An echo of an image? An image memory? A simple, inconspicuous moss.

That evening, the red skin rash returned, this time on my upper arms. I had better not drink milk. Or is it to do with Franz, who cools his arm in the water of the quarry pond?

THE AUTUMN ARRIVES in precipitous haste, as though it wants to make clear that its mercifulness was the reason for the unusually

KLAUS MODICK

mild late summer that lasted deep into October. Violent rainstorms and the first overnight frosts leave the foliage scarcely any time to turn color before the fall. It is as if someone has overslept and, upon waking too late, breaks through the closed door in a hectic rush.

Next to not being punctual, which he took as a personal insult, my father hated nothing more than unkempt, tangled hair and dirty fingernails. If he caught us in such a state, especially at the dinner table, he cried out, "That is the wilderness!" Or, in what amounted to an intensification: "That is decadence!"

By way of punishment, he then ordered us into the bathroom, reached for the terribly dull nail scissors, and cut our nails so short that often blood flowed from them. He proceeded similarly with everything that grew around the Mollberg house. His archenemy, the moss, was going to be made to see reason; it was time to "cut back and clear out." Branches, twigs, grasses that dared get too close to the walls would, with enormous hedge trimmers, with saw, ax, and hatchet, be "called to order." The branches of the pine, which kept knocking on the upstairs window because of the wind, once agitated him so severely that he wanted to cut down the whole tree. Mother was able to dissuade him only with great difficulty.

His compulsion to bring nature under control took on, at times like this, manic-paranoid characteristics. If foliage piled up around the house, mixing into wet clumps that began to decay, then the "hour of truth" arrived for the stiff besom brooms that we used. These had to keep the "goo," "the mud slide," "the slime," "the whole foliage tripe" away from the foundation, floor, and frame of the house.

"Moisture," groaned my father, "moisture is malicious. Moisture creeps in."

In order to understand his deep-seated disgust at all soil-created decay, you needed to have heard with what repugnance he let this phrase "moisture creeps in" fall from his lips. At the end of the summer holiday, before we could return to the city again, everything in the house that seemed even remotely capable of contributing to the creeping of the moisture had to be soaked with huge quantities of foul-smelling wood preservatives.

"*Similia similibus curantur*," he said, quoting the basic idea of homeopathy—that "likes are cured by likes"—as Franz and I waded into the stinking Xylamon solution. The only time my father ever struck me resulted from this situation. For I had suggested that he go ahead and drink the wood preservative himself if it was so important to him.

He certainly did not have the ambition of

civilizing the woods around the house into a park or garden. To the contrary, he was fixated on preserving the natural structure and traditional appearance of the bushy moorland that had emerged here over the course of a few decades from neglected, economically degraded pastureland. This purism, which was constantly refreshed through regular reading of works by Hermann Löns, led to a paradox: The immediate environment of the house was a well-tended forest, an area from which my father banished everything that in his view diluted the natural impression of a bush heath. When Franz once buried a few chestnuts in the autumn, which sprouted the following spring, my father tore out the seedlings—for him alien invaders—without further ado.

Nowadays the oaks, which were once kept bushy artificially, have grown up into stout trees; all manner of wild grasses, mosses, and flowers grow everywhere in the heather; and the besom brooms stand under a thick tissue of spiderwebs in the shed. There are three zones, as it were, in this shed. In the first lie, as ever, the firewood and coals. The second houses the work tools used by my brother's family. The third consists of the workbench that my father set up there. Strangely, neither my brother nor my nephew has altered anything in this corner of the shed. It gives off in its museumlike unreality an aura that has no other function than to whisper to the intruder a quiet yet energetic *Touch me not*. When I retrieved some coal from the shed earlier, the reflected light of stray sunbeams, which the clouds of the autumn sky released, passed through the dim window above this altar to my father's fanaticism for order. The work tools, arranged by size, hang in a straight line on the wall. Nails and screws lie in tin cans, each neatly marked with their respective lengths. Under the table, more canisters of Xylamon stand strictly aligned. The shelf holds, in rank and file, a parade of paint cans and brushes of various kinds.

But when I let my gaze linger a little on this statuelike sterility, I felt that something had escaped from this whole grotesque arrangement of bureaucratic accuracy, that this rigid order had shifted into an endlessly drawn-out process of disintegration. Dust and rust are the media of this patient decomposition, this decadence of the inorganic, this composting of the technological. Ax and hatchet and saw rot like the tree trunks that they cut. Shovel and spade become the soil that they shifted, brooms the mud that they swept. And over all lies the dust, like a moss of dryness.

PLAINS OF MOSS. HORIZONLESS. Heavenless. Walking in encircling greenery. Giant cats, on the hunt, pursue me. Darwin sits in a tree and shows the way with his waving beard. Wading breathlessly through bright red fields of clover with heart-shaped leaves. The cats lose the scent. The highest leaves of the plants reach my chest. The leaves are triangular, like my own heart.

Each leaf is designed precisely like a heart, in the color of the actual flesh. Fleshy stems fan the cooling wind. The fields undulate, begin to flow, pulling me along. In the masses of clover I flow toward nowhere, pulsating. The clover stems pass through me. Pumping evenly. But suddenly—cascades. The red river falters. Foam. Contraction. Anxieties. Breathlessness. The wood sorrel juts out from the whirlpool, wide at the ends, split in the middle, and pointed toward the stem. Darwin's beard beckons.

I open my mouth wide, for my extremities are rigid, motionless; I bite into a huge sorrel leaf, finding a hold. The red stream pulls away beneath me. Again the undisturbed pumping. A pecking sound sneaks up on me, growing ever louder, a nervous unrhythmic ticking. A tocking. The pecking, the ticking begin to race. My heartbeat cannot keep up the pace. The secondhand drives it mercilessly onward. From out of the ticking come the green lights of distant sea beacons. The second hand senselessly races around its circle.

When I look at my watch, it is the middle of the night. I take off the watch, but sleep does not want to return. My heart beats evenly. I hear it inside me. Clover with heart-shaped leaves. Wood sorrel. In homeopathy, they are prescribed for heart trouble. As in a dream, causality is twisted. Or set right. The nebulous yet often also precise perceptions, observations, feelings of dreams give rise to phenomena that one, in a waking state, would view as their cause. My heart warns me about the watch. Clover with heart-shaped leaves, wood sorrel. Darwin points where? Everything is connected with everything else. All things belong together.

Blood flows through the brain. Clover with heart-shaped leaves, wood sorrel, clover. A giant circulatory system. Cats on the hunt. A single in breath. An out breath. Why clover? Darwin studied clover. Why was that? An in breath and an out breath. An ecological circulatory system. Clover. Evenly pumping. Cats. Causality. Darwin. Circulation. Sleep does not want to come. Outside, a cat on the hunt prowls around. Its cries. Clover, cats, causality. The cat hunts field mice. Cycle. Field mice destroy bumblebee nests. Clover. Bumblebees pollinate the clover. That is the entry point, and this is how the elements of the cycle are linked together. It all comes back to me.

Darwin determined that only bumble-bees visit the red clover blossoms; other bees do not come around for their nectar. But if the bumblebee were to die out or become more scarce, says Darwin, the clover would also be encountered less frequently or would disappear altogether. How many bumblebees there are in a particular area depends in large part on how many field mice live there, since the mice destroy the bees' nests and sources of honey. But the number of field mice depends fundamentally on the number of cats who hunt in the area. Bumblebee nests are found most often in proximity to human settlements and small villages; their whereabouts can be attributed, in turn, to the large number of cats that subsist on the field mouse population and thereby keep it in check. Thus the presence of cats determines, indirectly, whether particular plants will flourish in a particular area, by affecting the size of the mice and bumblebee populations.

The clover that can vigorously propogate itself, thanks to the bumblebees and also the cats, serves as pasture for cattle. Sailors require large quantities of pickled beef. Accordingly, England can thank cats for its sea power. It can also thank older, unmarried women of England, with their boundless love of cats. Even as naval power led England into war and took men away from women, it produced a multitude of English women who, in the absence of marriage partners, fell in love with cats. The cats, however, keep the mice in check, to the benefit of the bumblebees, and back again to the beginning. That was the circle—a curious history. It was the classical history of the ecological cycle. Mandelbaum enjoyed telling it. Always from the beginning. Always in a circle. He lovingly embellished this story with details.

"Do you have it, Ohlburg? A cycle. No beginning, no end. Everything is one. Do you understand?"

The second hand chases my heart. But why do I need a watch here? When I leave it off for two days, the automatic mechanism comes to a halt. It stops. The thought makes me tired. Then sleep comes. Dreamless. Deep. I am asleep.

I no longer wear a watch.

MINE WERE THE TYPICAL SYMPTOMS of a cold—swollen nasal mucous membranes and increased production of mucus, which during the day lodged itself in the frontal sinus cavity and during the night, when I reclined, dissolved and ran down. But from the start, I had believed all this was instead an allergic reaction, of the sort that I had already become somewhat accustomed to from the climate systems in American houses. Either way, the condition was more than just an inconvenience. It created a feeling of pressurized closedness in my head; this muddled my powers of hearing and also my concentration, if I can label as concentration the considerably weakened attention I devoted to things at that time. I experienced a deadening of my entire sensorium; day after day, I had the feeling that I was packed in cotton, looking out at what enclosed me but without being able to get any closer to the surrounding environment.

It was all the more numbing since in recent weeks I believed that I had observed myself to be—half willingly, half compulsorily—in a kind of harmonious interplay with the world of appearances. I noticed these coincidental encounters with the world of objects because I began to experience that world unquestioningly, freed from the pressures of causality

and logical analysis. In any case, the illness-
induced sealing off of my head hindered any
further advances into this domain; gradually,
progressing in waves, it took over my whole
body. My taste buds largely failed to do their
duty, my glasses could no longer fully correct
my weak vision, and even my sense of touch
was diminished in a frightening way. Once I
dropped a cup of tea, because I believed that
I had a firm grip on it, whereas in reality I
had scarcely touched it at all.

I had almost decided to consult the physician in Wiefelstede, when a technological
failure presented a solution to—and relief
from—these circumstances. At the onset of
the heating season, I had only ever made
use of the electric heating system that Franz
had had installed some years earlier. Feed-
ing the old tiled stove seemed to me too
complicated and inconvenient. The electric
heating, however, operates via a principle of

nighttime storage and gives off heat during the day only if one adjusts it appropriately at night. One evening, I had forgotten to set the circuit breaker before going to bed, with the result that the next day the heating elements radiated only cold air. I therefore turned off the system and with quite some difficulty got the tiled stove to work.

When my coldlike symptoms did not act up this day, but, rather, suddenly disappeared, I did not at first attribute my improvement to this change in heating methods. But when on the following day I switched on the electric heating, now properly recharged, my symptoms returned with undiminished severity. In order to assure myself on this point, I turned the heat on and off a few times at half-hour intervals, and my body responded immediately. Presumably, the reason for this change is that the heating system's blower stirs up the house dust and triggers my reactions.

The symptoms, in any event, have not reappeared since, and just in case, I still heat the house only with wood and coal. So it will not do, after all, to speak of using the stove as an annoying, troublesome business.

In fact, I experience a feeling of deep satisfaction when, three or four times per day, I must go back and forth between the shed and the house in order to provide for my own heat. Despite its low heat value, wood has become for me far preferable to coal. When I load thick pieces of wood in my arms in order to carry them back to the house, an agreeable warmth already radiates out of them. When they then burn and, crackling, broadcast their new condition through the oven tiles, these waves of warmth resonate with the clear signals of a speechless form of communication. The fundamental distinction between burning, on the one hand, and heating with something, on the other hand, is now clear to me.

I heat with the wood, and the wood heats for me. As I gratefully acknowledge its friendly service, its warmth imparts to me the feeling of a wholly unfamiliar well-being.

Sometimes, though, it makes me sad that I have not known, not seen, not cut down myself the trees that undergo this transformation from a luscious green to a red-hot vital force, giving life. I frequently sit with my back leaning against the oven and listen to the singing of the logs inside. Some days, keeping the house heated with wood occupies me completely, the process taking up so much of my time and energy. Before I throw a piece of wood through the oven's hatch, I take it in hand, feel it, observe it with the greatest interest. No one piece looks like another—a banality that has been banal for so long that it is no longer recognized as such. Yet the variety, particularly of burl wood, is more than astounding. I attempt to

estimate the age of the wood by reconstruct-
ing the size of the trees, their double life in
earth and air, their simultaneous upward and
downward growth. Now and then I chew
small pieces of bark, especially ones that
already have moss attached to them.

A piece of root, to which I had at first
paid little attention, was too bulky to pass
through the oven hatch. I set it down on
the floor in front of my feet and observed
it in the encroaching twilight. Shaped like a
slingshot, its form reminded me vaguely of a
straddle-legged person standing there, especially since the thick upper end resembled a
head. The surface was fuzzy, frayed out into
various threads, beardlike. For a moment I
believed I had a mandrake root before me,
except that it was too large.

The more intensely I observed the root,
the clearer its appearance became; however,
when I squinted slightly, it seemed to look

back at me. Eventually, it occurred to me to remove my glasses. For a moment I saw myself in a half-blind mirror, saw myself in front of me, lying with splayed-out legs, but also saw myself sitting bent over me. This perception lasted perhaps only a fraction of a second, but it had an inner duration that belonged to an altogether different system for timekeeping. I did not want to burn this piece of root; instead, I picked it up, went outside, and searched in the woods for an appropriate place to put it, which I thought I found under a birch tree with two trunks. I laid it there in the moss.

When I passed by this spot a few days later, I noticed that the root was now a cushion of white moss, of the sort that is commonly used as an ornament for wreath making and in cemeteries.

THE CLEAR, SNOWLESS COLD PREVAILS, dry and quiet. Around midday the sun appears with surprising strength. I have made it a habit to take my midday rest in a recliner on the balcony, wrapped up, onionlike, in many layers of blankets. The balcony is open to the south, but its other sides are closed and roofed over. On the glass wall of the east side, ice flowers are to be found every morning. This astonishing phenomenon proves that talk of inanimate matter is mere nonsense: even the stars of ice mimic vegetative forms. At midday, when these living ornaments collapse into the humus of the meltwater, a pleasant accumulation of heat develops here, the sensation of which is all the more comfortable when I can feel and see the cold that encloses this winter greenhouse.

During this time, I feel like a cell pulsating with heat in the midst of a polar hostility to life, like life as such within an eternal icescape, and at first I spent these hours reading T. F. Thiselton-Dyer's *The Folk-lore of Plants*. This work is, it must be said, marked by a rare sensitivity toward the indefinable. But even it painfully demonstrates how much harder the disappointment hits us, the more we strain the spirit, stretch the intellect, augment our information, and refine our methods of inquiry in attempts to corral the wondrous. Yesterday, when I set the book down yet again in order to reignite my extinguished pipe, I inadvertently inhaled the tobacco smoke very deeply, which is not customary for me and which immediately created a swirling dizziness in my head. I exhaled the smoke forcefully and expansively; it combined with my frozen breath and developed into an impressive cloud. I leaned back and followed the figure of the white floating image in the still air. It moved off toward the group of three spruce trees that are about as old as I am. My father planted them himself, with the assistance of Franz and me. It appeared to me as though the spruces, for their part, drew toward them the smoke that I had pushed out with my breath. In constantly changing movements and formations, very much like a dance, it played around the boughs and branches of the small group of trees, rising and falling as it leisurely drew itself between and through them.

In the rhythm of the figures that formed there, an intuition touched me suddenly, like a wing beat; it far exceeded the limits of my field of research—indeed, extended far beyond my capacity for imagination more generally. It is impossible for me as a musical dilettante to describe this intuition, which in this moment revealed areas that otherwise only music, if anything, could penetrate: the weightless no-man's-land or, better put, the land for all that lies between immediate sensory intuition and intellectual, reflective reality. Between these poles shimmered alluringly, almost like a panderer, each smoke image, and if I cannot reconstitute in writing the immediacy of my experience of this group of trees and their dialogue with the white traces of my breath, I at least want to try to remember the dimensions of knowledge that passed before my mind during these few seconds. Perhaps the process of writing it down will bring back an echo of the immediacy in question.

Reading Thiselton-Dyer's work may have contributed to the way that everything appeared in a limitless simultaneity before my mind's eye—all of what I, from my childhood up until this moment, had absorbed while reading about plant mythology and plant cults. My account, which must necessarily be presented successively, will in no way do justice to the crowded contiguity and interpenetration of the images I remembered. Perhaps, however, my limitations can be overlooked. I am not a poet. And indeed, long before a poet like Ovid spoke of Philemon and Baucis, myths, sagas, and recollections of plant metamorphoses were found in the history and the representational worlds of all peoples, all cultures.

Narcissus is the best known, and the most fascinating. Phoroneus was the son of a tree nymph, and Attis came from an almond. Myrrha was changed into myrrh. Even Jupiter was once a tree, and the Egyptian goddess Hathor is supposed to have emerged from a mighty trunk. Hesiod believed that humans had developed from the seed of the ash tree; Homer said it was the seed of the oak. In India, the fig tree is held to be the cradle of humankind. According to the Nordic sagas, the whole of humanity stems from the ash and the elm trees. Our word *ash* comes from the Nordic *aska*, which means "man." Yggdrasil, the world-spanning ash tree, was sacred to Odin, because its roots reached out into the universe.

And Yggdrasil was itself rooted in the tree of life from the book of Genesis, from whose roots in turn the Kabbalah's tree of life sprouted—the tree of life that bears the pomegranates in which the Star of David lies embedded, as can be seen when the fruits are cut open. The Christian God died on tree wood formed into a cross. On Borneo, the Dayaks worship the spirit of rice. The Polynesians pray to the soul of flower fragrances, while the Sinhalese say that the coconut palm will die of grief if it hears no human voice. The Miami Indians recognize the spirit of maize, and the Iroquois fear the spirit of the pumpkin. In Walachia, there is talk of the soul of the water lily. For their part, some Siamese people offer trees cakes and rice before cutting them down.

Artemis lived in a cedar, in a hazel bush, and in meadows. Athena dwelled in the olive tree. In the Persian pantheon, the cypress is the symbol of the ultimate, while Buddha was reincarnated forty-three times as a tree spirit before he experienced enlightenment as a human under the fig tree. As for oaks, it was not only the Celtic Druids who knew their power. Homer called them "the guarantor of safety." It was from their rustling leaves that the oracle of Dodona prophesied. Our word *church* comes from the Latin *quercus*, and hence the oak.

The oracular power of trees stems from their roots, which maintain a connection with the underworld. The Old Testament records numerous speaking trees: the magical oak near Sichem, the mulberry trees of David, the burning bush of Moses. And then there is the holy plane tree of Zarathustra in the Caucasus; the holy palm of the pre-Islamic Arabs in Nejran; the power of the laurel, which seers ate or smoked; the fig tree in whose place Rome was built; the lotus, which Egyptians, Indians, Tibetans, and Chinese sanctify as the seat of the most holy; the lilies of Hera, the roses in the groves of Diana, and the red anemone marking Adonis's death.

All of this stems from, roots itself in, and is interwoven with these three spruces, which have lived for about as long as I have. And when the smoke had dissolved into the night, I continued to stare into these spruces. All that I had known in these moments about the secret of trees, of plants, I felt and experienced—but not via this poor enumeration of this, that, and the other. Rather, all of it got entangled, became intertwined, knotted together, simultaneously and infinitely, brightly and lightly. But it disappeared with

the smoke. Only the spruces remained. I
tried to remember the magic of the Christ-
mases of my childhood, but it did not return
to me, did not want to come into my head. I
tried, but I could not make it come.

Now, as I try to put down on paper the
memory of this event, I am struck by the
irony that to my knowledge moss never was
anything other, was never considered as anything other, than what it always was and is
and will be: moss. Perhaps the mosses have
their seeming inconspicuousness, which I
begin to see through, to thank for this: Their
low growth, and the concealed place that
they seek out in surrounding vegetation, has
excited the curiosity neither of collectors
nor of botanists. They are, as plants, without
secrets. And even the mythological, occult
thinking that has covered almost every other
plant with magical or symbolic meanings
forgot the mosses. They have no nutritional

value and no toxic effects. Only sometimes, I believe, have they taken on poetic significance. Their only use is indeed their uselessness, although they are not really ornamental plants. They are probably so beautiful because that is *all* they are: beautiful.

And yet there must be something more to moss—something that attracts me, involves me. Something that drives the moss to approach me. But what? I know—or rather, I knew the answer once. But when?

ALONG WITH MILDER COLD, a snowy new year has arrived. Yesterday Franz, his wife, Marianne, their son, Peter, and their five-year-old daughter, Claudia, all left. They have been visiting with me during the week between Christmas and New Year's to celebrate the holiday in a natural setting with their daughter—but probably also, as Franz remarked with somewhat awkward irony, to check whether the old emeritus is coping as a hermit. I can't say that I felt bothered by the visit, and I have actually enjoyed the days spent with family. But now that I am alone once again, I feel liberated. Although I have been throughout my life a gregarious person who enjoys discussion and debate, the sudden presence of five people, the ringing out of five different voices, awoke in me on several occasions a disturbing sense of strain, as though it had become difficult for me to look at anything, to listen to anything.

That said, it was very pleasant to have the management of the household chores taken out of my hands for once. As an old bachelor, I am accustomed to performing these daily tasks, but in the past weeks I have felt increasingly weaker, physically speaking. It was only the care of the tiled stove that I refused to relinquish, although I did name little Claudia as my assistant and initiated her, to her great enthusiasm, in the secrets of the oven fire. She handled the wood extremely carefully, without my having to admonish her.

Marianne and Franz, who is a longtime hobby chef, took over the kitchen. All sorts of meat was served. I refrained from any discussion of that issue, not only to avoid disturbing the peace but also because, to my own surprise, meat once again tasted good to me. For years I had dropped it almost completely from my diet; here in Mollberg, I renounced it entirely. I have never stopped to consider why that was so. My need for meat seemed simply to fade away. I did not have ethical motives; indeed, as I write these words I am struck by the thought that an ethical vegetarianism probably can only emerge from an ignorance of nature, for whoever does not want to sink his teeth into the flesh of animals must sink his teeth into other sorts of living organisms.

Christmas Eve was lovingly orchestrated for the child. From the table, we could see out into the cluster of spruces. I had trimmed the middle tree, the largest of the three, and it seemed to take joy from this, if I may so interpret the fact that its branches reached directly toward me. Claudia was visibly impressed that Christmas trees grow in the forest and therefore need not be thrown into the trash on New Year's. Right away she wanted to know why this specific tree— and here she pointed toward the decorated spruce—and not another—here she gestured toward a bare oak—could be the Christmas tree.

"Because it is green even in the winter," said Peter, naturally provoking Claudia's next question—namely, why it remained green even in the winter.

"No," Franz said. "You must ask Uncle Lukas that question. He knows all about it."

And I actually began to lecture the child, talking nonsense. Although I tried to avoid technical terms as much as possible, I noticed how little by little Claudia's interest waned, how a great disappointment came over her face, as I talked about the way the chlorophyll split the sunlight like a transparent pane of glass that is colored green, absorbing the red and blue light waves while letting the green pass through; the way the solar energy absorbed in this manner is not transformed into heat but, rather, brings about a simple chemical reaction, whereby water, mineral salts, and carbon dioxide from the atmosphere combine and thereby form living matter as well as sugar, which enables the cells to build up stable membranes and create food reserves. But as the terms for the tree—*common spruce* or *Picea abies*—spilled out, verbatim, from my lips, I broke off uneasily. The child was still looking at me, but the irrepressible curiosity in her eyes had given way to a disbelief that seemed almost angry.

"No," Claudia said resolutely when I fell silent. "No, Uncle Lukas. You are lying."

"Please, Claudia. You shouldn't say such things."

Marianne looked at me apologetically.

"Claudia is right," I murmured. "It may all really be completely different, totally otherwise."

Looking for help, I stared at something absent in the group of spruces, something that had once already shown me how everything is indeed completely different. The Christmas tree in the middle seemed to lean toward me in the wind, seemed to want, once again, to unlock memories, to provide signs that I could understand, that I could read in the tree and its movements, that I needed only to read out loud to the child.

"In fact, it's like this."

And I read the story of Attis, the son of the Phrygian Nana; Attis had castrated himself (I said merely that a wound had been inflicted) and he lay dying under a spruce tree when Cybele, mother of the gods, found him there. She prevented his death by transforming him into the tree, and made Zeus promise that the tree would remain forever green. From Attis's blood, violets are supposed to have grown, and for the spring festival dedicated to Cybele, a fir or a spruce was felled, wrapped in cloths, decorated with violets, and then carried into the Phrygian sanctuary. On the third day (but I read this silently to myself, because I believed that it might be unsettling to Claudia), the day of blood, the priests, all eunuchs, inflicted wounds on themselves.

The ecstasy of the cult reached such a pitch that the men castrated themselves.

"Ah, yes." Franz laughed. "Our great book of myths and sagas. Now it all comes back to me again. We got that from Father one Christmas. Yes, it's great that you remember it. My impression was that all you think about these days is your terminology."

"I think about that, too, my dear brother."

Claudia was now very happy. We exchanged gifts, small ones, though even here the web of relationships from recent months did not let me down, for I received a picture book with the title *Ancient Trees in Middle Europe*. Claudia wanted to know why one received gifts only on Christmas, but before Marianne and Peter could respond with a gently educational rebuke, the spruces had gotten hold of me again.

"There is another old story about that. Once in the Harz, some young girls were

Klaus Modick

dancing around a spruce in which a gob-
lin had hidden. They wanted to cut off his
escape route with their dance and demanded
that he give them gifts for his freedom."

"How do you know all this?" Claudia
asked.

Even Franz was amazed that I still knew
all these stories.

"These are stories," I said happily, "that
the Christmas tree has told me."

Claudia was astonished. We laughed.

"You are a regular fairy-tale uncle," Peter
said wonderingly. "I would not have believed
you were an old man of science at all."

"The older one becomes, the better one
can remember."

"Well," said Franz, "I don't know about
that."

WHILE CLAUDIA AND HER ELDER BROTHER
used the frozen lake to try out the skates
they had been given for Christmas, Franz
and I took once again our old route through
the Henntings' pastures in the direction of
Spohle. No snow had fallen yet, but it was
in the air. A pale sun hung motionlessly over
the frozen-solid expanses, on which now, in
the early afternoon, isolated patches of mist
still lay or were already re-forming. Franz,
who at the end of this summer term would
become an emeritus professor himself, held
nothing back about how very disconcert-
ing his recent years at the university had
been. In the late 1960s, he had, though not
without inner resistance, adopted aspects of
a reconceived psychology; as he began to
grasp that even this science might be embedded in social relationships and interests, he
asked not only about its proper subject matter but also, increasingly, about its political

functions. And now, scarcely a dozen years later, a new irrationalism had broken out at the university, an irrationalism that could be considered romantic and green in color, and from which psychology was by no means spared. For example, Nietzsche was now in all seriousness viewed as a significant psychologist, despite his influence on the political history of which our family had had such bitter experience.

"In one of my last seminars with students, some of whom I esteemed very highly"—and here Franz spoke as though he were still stunned, shaking his head—"in a discussion about theories of memory, the claim was actually made that the functions and structures of memory, its mechanisms, could be much more fully clarified by reading certain novels than through psychology or psychoanalytic theory. Imagine that, Lukas. Imagine that someone in the field of botany stood up and opined that one could acquire better observations and more information about the flora of Ammerland if, instead of using a microscope, one consulted an effusive nature poem about violets in springtime or I know not what. Nothing against literature. But everything in its proper time. Everything in its proper place."

"That's something Father could have said," I remarked, in order to evade Franz. With a sleepwalker's certainty he had plucked a string that months ago began to vibrate ever more strongly within me. Did he suspect something about my circumstances? Did he wish to provoke me?

"Well," Franz said, pushing the topic aside, "it's all the same to me. All that is behind me now. And you? Are you making progress with your critique?"

"Do you see that group of birches over there?" I pointed ahead toward them.

"Yes, of course. What of it?"

"It is very lovely. Can one say more? I have stopped asking myself why it is there, why in general anything is there. The answer is always only because. And this line of questioning distracts me."

Franz gave me a suspicious sidelong glance.

"Distracts you? From what?"

"It is impossible to state that," I said.

Franz laid his hand gently on my shoulder. He was really concerned about me, because we had always, in all other circumstances, avoided touching each other.

"Lukas, old boy, are you sure you're feeling well? Will you be all right here, all alone? You are no longer the youngest. Come back with us. You ought to be among people again."

"You don't need to worry about me. I'm absolutely fine. Occasionally, I do get terribly tired. But if I were around more people, I might feel that way even more often. Here I'm able to get my work done. My critique of terminology grows and thrives, though it blooms in ways that I could not have anticipated. It is almost running riot, if you will."

Franz tried to give our conversation an ironic twist.

"Is that the reason why you have grown this beard?"

"Exactly. My beard is the moss of old age. You should grow one, as well. It keeps one warm."

This made me chuckle. Franz looked at me again, concerned, unsettled, but held his peace. We tramped wordlessly through the deeply frozen grass, until Spohle emerged ahead of us from the thick, dense mist.

"Let's turn back," Franz suggested. "It's getting dark."

"How about a small beer and schnapps at the tavern?"

"Father could have said that."

We laughed.

"Cools in the summer, warms in the winter," said the innkeeper, as he served us a corn liquor and beer.

"'But it is moist. And moisture, boys, moisture creeps in!'"

Here I quoted Father. Franz nearly choked with laughter.

"Okay, then, cheers!"

We drank and inspected each other.

"And what," Franz suddenly asked, "do you do with your time when you're not working on your manuscript?"

"I dream."

"I see. And of what?"

"Difficult to say."

"Come on, tell me. This is finally something that falls within my domain of expertise."

"I don't want to have my dreams inter-preted. For me, dreams and waking are melting into one another more and more. I no longer know where my dreams begin and where they end. In fact, I don't even want to know."

"Lukas, is everything really okay with you?"

"Things have never been better. But if it will reassure you, I will gladly tell you about one of my dreams. I had it yesterday, or the day before yesterday, or even earlier. Maybe I won't dream it until tomorrow. What differ-ence does it make? It's all the same, equally valid. That's just the way it is.

"I'm standing at the edge of a huge corn-field, which is bordered by an endlessly wide veldt. There is a rustling in the cornfield. I'm startled. I see a man step out of the field, moving out into the veldt. I know him, even know his name. I call out to him. But he doesn't react, his movements being quite stiff and jerky. I approach him, shake him by the arm, look into his wide-open saucerlike eyes. They are like the eyes of someone who has been hypnotized, or who is in a severe state of shock. I call out his name again. Again he does not react. He just moves stubbornly onward, like a robot.

"He carries a rucksack and has something of the soldier about him. Suddenly a thought occurs to me. I command him, as one commands a soldier in a drill. 'Forward! Stand still! Hit the deck! Up!' He does all this obediently, but still in a trance, still with the abrupt movements of an automaton. Suddenly he awakens, points with his hand into the veldt in panicked shock. I look in that direction, from which three tanks are closing on us. 'Hit the deck! Take cover! Quiet!' I shout. They don't notice us. But he has already pulled out a hand grenade and he throws it in front of the tanks, because of which they take notice of us, turn toward us, pursue us. Now I, too, throw a hand grenade, which hangs from my belt, and as both grenades explode in quick succession, we run for our lives to the cornfield.

"The tanks open fire, but we reach, unhurt, the protective green of the field. As we bolt into the cover, we are only one person. The stranger has entered into me. I hasten breathlessly through the swaying green, where a few places are already smoldering, already burning; I seek protection and safety. And as I hurry through the green, flames shooting up from everywhere, suddenly I can fly. I float over the sea of corn and watch, singing a hymn about the beauty of the fields. As I try to swat at a mosquito whining around my head, I wake up."

Franz ordered a second round and we drank to each other. He kept quiet a few minutes, nodded to himself as though he understood, and then began, as though speaking to himself, to draw associations.

"Veldt: bleakness, emptiness, death. Cornfield, green: life. Robot, soldier: the domain of the orderly, science; tank: danger . . ."

"Franz, I don't want any interpretations. No analyses."

"That is not an analysis. If you were not the person I know, I would say that you in your strict disciplinarity have become ever more distanced from life, from greenness; that you are marching right toward an emptiness; that you are not listening to yourself; that you are even conjuring danger, putting yourself at risk. But you can still turn back, although your situation is already extremely urgent. And you realize this, start to live again. But why should you be afraid? Indeed, you as a botanist have been, for your whole life, closer to the green than any of us. Perhaps—"

"Franz! Leave me be. Let it be simply thus, as it is."

He remained silent, but I noticed his growing uneasiness. He was concerned about me. I really liked him, and in this moment he was perhaps dearer to me than ever—and yet I wished that he would just leave me alone.

"But will you have another round with your little brother, or not?"

We laughed, drank up, and made our way home. Arm in arm, we took the road back, for we would have stumbled in the dark fields. The tapping of our feet on the frozen street, the stiff bricks. We walked at the same pace, he and I. In the same silence.

THEY HAVE LEFT AGAIN. I remain. It was a stopping point between stations. Someone has checked my ticket, but he could not make out my destination. My journey continues.

It is a slow fall. Sometimes, though, it is a rising upward.

SKIES SUCH AS THIS just have to be blue, with fleecy white clouds. Above everything, in the far west, five radiant fingers reach out, sedately, from the egg-yolk yellow sun. If you look into the sun long enough, you begin to see her broad smile. Or, standing upside down, you would be able to discern her grief at having to die every night. Pleasantly, at my age one no longer feels the need to stand on one's head or walk on one's hands. So it is the eternally smiling kindness of the full, the single truth, that remains.

In the distance behind, to the east, are peaks and steep mountainous areas visibly covered in gray snow. I'm almost ashamed to admit that up to now I have never noticed them. It is possible that I, at Claudia's age, also knew about this mountain range and saw it, but I've lost the ability to spread myself out across the earth, to take everything into myself. Lately, though, there are more and more moments in which I put my feet in the moss or look into the sun with half-closed eyes, and then, a breeze blowing some-where far off, the earth gives way beneath me, becomes small—becomes, again, a star. In this winter sky, which wears the colors of summer, the stars are falling.

If it were nighttime, the stars might have six points, the moon appearing as a sickle with the same yellow color that the sun had. But as it is, the five wide beams reach out—beams that are excluded from the visible ter-ritory of the sun—such that everything can be observed in a never-before-seen light. The house stands exactly in the middle, but it occupies only a very small part of the whole. The roof and its environs project such a

confidently continuous red that one does not
see the moss encroaching on them. Even the
wooden walls have that same strong brown
color that they had when they were first built;
they show no trace of weathering. The door
is simply a huge black cavity, and the windows
are blue like the sky. The balcony in the attic,
my wintertime greenhouse, my heating cell,
captures, in a way that seems more real than
the real thing, the full, unclouded color of
the sun. Thick gray smoke pours out of the
chimney, becomes subtilized as it is drawn up
into the blue sky, and, by the time it reaches
the distant mountains, appears as only a thin
curvy line, a pencil mark on the horizon.

Apart from the treatment of the sky and
the house, an orgy of green and brown undu-
lates over and through the greatest part of the
surface. Out of this apparent flux, where the
rigid uprightness of the leafless trees towers
into the sky and the wide-reaching arms of

the evergreens meet the blank whiteness, an innocent knowledge of detail jumps out at me. This knowledge comes not from studying, but, rather, from a great sense of wonder— from the wonder that anything, anything at all, exists. And that it is beautiful. The frost-stiffened forest, through whose trees one can see so far during this time of year, appears to me not dead, but, rather, sleeping. And in the forest's dreams reigns a life force that desires to burst through, an agitated kind of life whose expression in the lines, strokes, and surfaces has become solidified without being dead. Near the lower border, which is completely dominated by the darkest shade of green, a man lies stretched out. His long beard, in color and movement the same as the wood smoke that flows from the chimney, forces its way up like a root through the green ground—and on out of the picture.

"That's you, Uncle Lukas," Claudia had

said when she gave me her crayon picture as she was leaving.

"And where, exactly, am I?"

"In the moss. All the moss. Don't you see that?"

Oh, yes, I do see. I see it ever more clearly. This picture hangs over my writing desk, right next to the window. If I alternately observe the picture and then look out the window, it seems to me as if the picture were a window in its own right. It offers a view of reality, an insight into nature, from whose powerful vastness, which is at the same time an extraordinarily intimate proximity, the glass window separates me, functioning as a cloudy filter between me and the forest. The truth of this child's drawing lies in its memorylessness. Yet the naïveté is complicated, and the absence of memories discloses an immense power of recollection. Claudia's thoughtful, almost refined way of approaching me is evident here—her delightful air of haughty charm and uncompromising grace, the way she was incorruptible when I lectured her about chlorophyll at Christmas. The child knows what is of and in nature, and can still grasp it as a whole, including mountains that we no longer see. The child can say something about death as the price of life—and show this by drawing me in the moss.

Evolutionarily considered, moss, in fact, has no future; one could say that it is always only pondering its own past. Its present, however, is pure, humble beauty. As rather regressive plants, mosses evolved from one of the simplified-to-the-essentials, long-ago-vanished primitive land plants, perhaps in the Tertiary period, perhaps earlier. Their sexual propagation reveals these connections very clearly, playing out exclusively in the medium of water. Moss thus reflects the age-old tendencies of its ancestors. But true regressions are unknown to evolution; the regression of moss is a simulated one, which has ensured its survival.

Life constantly uses reversions, harkening back, but it disallows truly retrograde movements, even if it often simulates them. Just as the regression of moss falls short of being an actual regression, so, too, will the old man who thinks childishly fall short of becoming a child again. Likewise the scientist whose thoughts are grown over with images will fall short of becoming a painter or—if his ideas are instead attacked by a kind of poetry—a writer.

Whenever I'm at the Hennting farm to buy supplies and pick up the mail that the country postman delivers there, ever since I told him it was not worth his while to make the detour to my place, especially in the snow, I stay for a half hour, more or less, sitting in the great kitchen and speaking with old Wilhelm Hennting, who has been around a dozen years longer than I. As the result of a stroke, he has been confined to a wheelchair for seven years; and as the result of a second stroke last spring, he has also become, as one says, confused. From time to time, however, clarity comes over him. He then recognizes me again, knows my name and remembers things and events that a younger person would already have forgotten long ago. I feel akin to him, though in the manner of a mirror image. His moments of clarity reveal thoughts that seem unclear to me, and in his absences of mind he perhaps gets closer to things than I can get through my considered reflections.

In any case, my family owes a lot to the old man. During our nearly fifty years of forced stays abroad, Hennting has, with a country person's guile and stubbornness, ensured that we were not dispossessed of our house in Mollberg. Shortly before our emigration, Father had officially transferred the house to him, and Wilhelm acknowledged the arrangement with an indefinable wink. He had never told us the details about how he convinced an expropriation-mad regime that the house was actually his own. His influence in this region, growing out of the four-hundred-year tradition of Henntings living on their farm, was evidently deeper than political power structures. In any case, in 1947 he handed over to us with great matter-of-factness the key and the deed to the house, refusing any form of payment. He never spoke of politics, but he made no secret of his contempt for National Socialism, which earned him more than a few friends in the neighborhood.

And so it surprised me all the more when during my latest visit, which found Hennting in a clear state of mind, he did not speak as usual about old times, good and bad harvests, or seed qualities; nor did he fulminate about the pernicious influence of technology on country life, one of his favorite subjects. Rather, he asked me directly what I thought of the political movement that designated itself as Green. He watched a lot of TV, such and such shows, not understanding much any longer; but he had picked up enough to realize that nowadays one could form a political party from the most obvious feature of the earth. Could it be that people had finally grasped that not politics but, rather, nature constitutes the true concern of humankind? But how, exactly, does one go about doing politics by means of nature? That may be the biggest piece of mischief. Of course, whoever destroys nature destroys him- or herself. But how could that issue be negotiated in parliament? The supporters of this new party would do better to come here for the harvest and lend a hand. An extra pair of arms would always be welcome.

Yet these young people knew absolutely nothing about what they romanticized. How can you talk about the environment, cleaner nature, pure eating, and so forth if you're speaking of matters of which you have no knowledge whatsoever? Did I believe, he asked, that even a single one of these Green youths knew how to milk a cow correctly? Or how to distinguish rye from oats, oats from wheat, wheat from barley, summer grains from winter grains, early sowing from late sowing? Did any of them know what an oak is? A birch? A spruce? For them, a tree is a tree, grain is grain, and if they ever heard a nightingale, they would probably think that it was a blackbird singing. What a joke!

They held seats now in parliaments, regional councils, local districts. Everywhere. They demonstrated against nuclear power. That was all well and good, but they probably did not even know how to work a wood-burning stove. At first, when the party bigwigs would come to the farm to solicit his vote, he told them that he had no time for politics. Eventually, though, he had to ensure that politicians got something to chew over. Some talk. Others do things. It has always been so. His son, who now managed the farm, slowly came to realize that all of the artificial fertilizers, the chemicals, were just a mess. They destroyed the soil, and the critters, as well. Then everything got out of balance. Everything. And it could never be set right again.

Before I could utter even a single word in reply, the old man's stream of speech dried up as suddenly as it had burst forth out of him. He stared sightlessly out of the window and

did not seem to register my parting saluta-
tion. Where had he gone? Not having to take
a stand on the issues he had raised, though,
was fine by me. The subject reminded me of
a disagreeable discussion that had taken place
among Peter, Franz, and me over Christmas.

Peter turned out to be, to Franz's great
anger, a member of the ecological movement, this being difficult to reconcile with
his neo-Marxist tendencies. Franz had held
forth in a very engaged manner, asserting
that this pseudopolitical movement heralded
the return of Luddism, irrationalism, nativ-
ism, and indeed blood-and-soil ideology. He
had attempted to entice me to break through
Peter's defenses, for he had counted on my
being, as a botanist, a capable ally. But I held
myself back—it may have been because I did
not want any hostility around me, or it may
have been because, like old Wilhelm, I cannot
or do not wish to grasp that our environment

is already so badly ruined that anyone with a commitment to it wins elections.

To the discussion at hand, I made only a single contribution, mentioning something I had read. Specifically, it has been observed of mosses that they develop astonishing capabilities of absorbing chemical substances in large quantities from the environment, sequestering and then ultimately neutralizing those substances. For example, radioactive waste originating from nuclear power plants has been found, concentrated 100,000-fold, in a moss native to France, *Cinclidotus danubicus*. Peter had expressed disgust about what that means. Did it therefore follow that this moss would soon be domesticated by us, as well? I replied by saying that I was surprised at the phenomenon but could not interpret it.

On my return from the Hennting farm, the matter kept going around in my head.

Maybe it signified nothing other than that mosses are waking up out of their evolution-ary dormancy and, in view of the destruction of the earth, the disappearance of humans, beginning a desperate attempt to put a stop to this destruction with their feeble means. Moss could be trusted to do that.

But my confidence in it is even stronger.

THE DAYS BECOME JUST BARELY perceptibly longer. The sun stands higher. My midday meditations on the balcony expand in time as well as space.

If one stares into the sun for a few moments with open eyes, as soon as one shuts them again, streaky patterns and shapes appear on one's retina. Most noteworthy are their motions, which flow out in all con-ceivable directions but without the patterns thereby losing their contours. A green circle grows, pulsating, out of a yellow one, which for its part flows out of a red one. It moves away from me but also enters into me; moves upward into my brain but at the same time remains near my lower eyelid; billows out on all sides and yet continues to hover, balloon-like, in the center—shrinking, growing, gestating, dying. As I try to adapt the movements of my mind to these shifts, which bring the dynamic into the static and the static into the dynamic, apparently irreconcilable elements are joined together in a flattened formation that creates an infinite expansion of space.

The body, my body, emulates these movements. It outgrows itself without departing from itself. I do not just sit on the balcony but also feel that I am sitting together with the balcony, the whole house, within the space of myself. I can reach the clouds. This unconditional and boundless mobility is not goal-directed; rather, it emanates from itself and melts down into every tiny particle of movement the movement of the whole. Is this like the bodily sensation, in the mother's womb, of the unborn child?

Childhood arrives and renounces the contracting impulses of concentration; it becomes lost in an indiscriminate melting away in all directions. Adulthood overcomes this condition, replacing the desire for boundlessness with a concentrated decision in favor of a few firmly held elements—a decision by means of which the mature individual achieves productivity. One no longer swims directionless in the great stream of the whole, going anywhere and everywhere; rather, one builds a filtering sieve through which that stream flows, and thereby attempts to catch the parts of reality that are necessary for the construction of personality. Hence adulthood is similar to the mouth of whales, through which masses of plankton are sieved, or even the formation of a reef, to which ever new corals of experience, knowledge, and memory cling, such that a person takes shape. Then in the conscious approach toward death, in becoming old and wanting to be, to remain alive, the circle is closed. The oversaturation with concentrated creation, with ideas and information, releases a new form of self-awareness—the awareness that the self can melt away again. In this closing of the circle, life achieves an apparent regression similar to the one that evolution brings about in the mosses.

My circumstances resemble ever more closely the patterns that form on my retina at night. Separations, distinctions, become impossible and meaningless. The I overlaps with the All. The All begins to moss over—to mossify—the I. The capacity to become similar becomes more powerful with each act of empathetic identification; it becomes the capacity to undergo metamorphoses and, finally, the ability to become interchangeable. And equally valid.

The similarity between humans and all of nature, as encoded in the myth and fable of the mandrake root, spreads from the appearance—the phenomenon—to language and thought. For the mandrake is really the omni-mandrake, the fundamental equivalence of all being. Ultimately, this impulse encompasses all conscious and unconscious functions, all aspects of the individual, until it is entirely equivalent even to what is opposed to it and everything can be anything. When I look at the pine tree or the moss, the plant gives me a kind of psychic charge, and if I have, in turn, charged it with myself, it mirrors me back again and I it. Thus the plant actually approaches me; it becomes an island in space, sees only me, becomes one with me. This is all so simple that it resists being described.

As I now write down the word *Moos*, as I have done so often before, my eyes and the two middle letters fall into one another. I drop into realms of dark green, swim through forests of algae from which the mosses evolved; sink into cells, bottle-shaped ducts; and penetrate, in the form of a colorless spermatozoa, to the tip of these bottlelike shafts. I push deeper, turn back again—my movement however always being directed forward as I search, in a stretched-out shape, through a structure that lacks cell walls. Ocean plankton rises, sinks back down; the blue of the sky disappears; the chlorophyll is gone; a gray veil of mist is everywhere. I assume the shape of a drop, waterlike; large white spots proliferate across a colorless sky; the canvas becomes visible, the blank paper, the coarsemeshed grid. The wind lifts me up. I drift, circling endlessly in the cool breath of the wind. Shady gray wisps of cloud. Softly falling crystals of snow. Look.

On the blanket lies snow. A moss of coldness. Snow glitters in my beard. My face burns in the chill air.

Where cushion mosses cover the ground, the winter holds off the March wind much longer. The melting has been oozing through the forest for days, laying bare the clamminess of it all. The long rigid freeze is loosened, as if with a smacking of the lips. There is a slow dripping from the roof—or rather, from everything in general. Rays of sunlight lick the remaining patches of snow. The wind lifts vaporous mists from the ground. The earth yawns and turns over in its sleep, stretching mightily. Joints of frost spring up like roots that had been deeply buried. In the sandy paths, these crusted clumps seep back into the ground as mud, in all its monotony. A release, a gentle pulling, a stretching, and the snow cover is rolled up.

The last white-gray pillows of snow cling to the moss in the tree limbs. Starlings swarm against the gray sky. Sometimes, between them, a track of blue appears. Something lifts. The grass gulps meltwater. The cold falls, powerless, from the pines, oaks, and birches. It trickles. It drips. The winter staggers. There is a thawing, a growing, a proliferation, a beckoning. A wind blows constantly. The winter disappears, and in its dwindling something swells. The pulse beats restlessly; the heart keeps false time.

I journey to Wiefelstede. The doctor listens. Nods his head. Listens. Taps. Nods his head.

"You already know what it is?"

I nod my head, tell him the name of the medicine I need. He nods his head, writes a prescription. The pharmacist cannot decipher what it says. I tell him the name of the medicine. He nods his head. Then, in the bakery, I order tea. Seven drops three times a day. A dripping, a thawing. It becomes quieter. I walk through the village, which is much changed.

The church stands in the middle, as it has for six hundred years. It has not changed. The foundation walls were hewn from granite boulders, reminders of the ice age. They are as high as my forehead. Piled up across them are weathered bricks, held in place with rusty wrought iron. And growing over all of it, moss. Over joints, crevices, cracks, and gaps.

The door is ajar, but I don't want to go inside. I remain outside; it is too early. The cemetery has a great beauty. It is taken care of but not worked on. It is left alone. Only where sites are freed up through decay is there space for new resting places. The centuries lie next to and on top of one another. But the marble stones disturb the peace. They are foreign; they will remain foreign. Their surfaces are completely smooth.

The rock mosses here settle only on the granite rocks, on the boulders from the ice age. They cover the surfaces with dark, almost black cushions. They love an erotics of death. And they live the erotics of erraticness, which outlasts death. In their growth, they track all the uneven areas in the stones' surface. They anchor themselves in—become almost inseparable from—the stone. They cover the pious sayings. They grow over the names. They spread out over the dates. They love very cold temperatures, yet they survive the summers. They go to sleep along with the winters, persevering in a patient stillness until the cold returns and they awaken. Then they once again extend out over the stones.

But they avoid the marble. They know that it comes from the south. It is too warm, too smooth, too youthful. The rock mosses love the cold. And the old. In the springtime they go to sleep.

Moss. Tomb of stones.

AS THE ROCK MOSSES FALL ASLEEP, to hibernate during the summer months, all the other mosses assess the state of the snowmelt for purposes of food intake, growth, and reproduction. One finds here biological and botanical evidence for the thermodynamic fact that water's melting point and freezing point are the same. The fact of this sameness is undeniable, even as a parallel fact remains inconceivable—namely, that love and death are also identical.

Ever since my sojourn to the cemetery, I have felt so healthy again, in the blossoming spring, that I face the prospect of my own death with great calmness. It is another indisputable fact that my good health is due to the heart medicine. But that doesn't explain my readiness for death—really, a kind of muted wishing for it. I have fallen in love with moss, and when I sense how this love is reciprocated, I yearn for the moment—without wanting to hasten its arrival artificially—when my increasing ability to be similar to moss, to undergo metamorphoses, will pass over into a pure identity, one no longer requiring interpretation.

The life of plants corresponds to the death, the being unborn, of humans. Moss lives only in the here and now, at the level of the group soul, the collective consciousness. It has refused individuation but thereby developed the maximum degree of living self-awareness. Thus it forms a fully autonomous, independent realm, hermetically separated from the animal world and yet unconnected to the rest of the plant world. Apart from preventing the soil from drying out, it is absolutely useless. That explains its singular beauty, whose use, though, is to reveal through its mere existence the uselessness of usefulness. In order to capture all this, one needs a way of observing and describing that makes transparent the impenetrability of science. Even as I hear the call for this kind of representation, I translate it, in turn, using my impenetrable terms, going around and around in a circle. That is the revenge of my lifelong botanical gaze.

In this science, arguably, the use of approximations is concealed. It thus leads up to the inexpressible that lies beyond the nameable, but never reaches it, does not recognize the name of what is nameless. This is particularly the case in our times because scientific knowledge expands ever faster and more comprehensively, at the largest as well as the smallest scales. The increase of knowledge does not reduce the puzzles, but, rather, multiplies them; does not illuminate the secret, but, rather, throws ever new veils over it. Every term for a new phenomenon, every answered question gives rise to a thousand new questions, and makes a thousand new terms necessary.

A tender science, if I may put it that way, must engage in a more rigorous search for beauty, which is like a moss of knowledge. It would then realize that beauty and truth are identical. In the botanist's piercing gaze, science only feeds on and exploits the fullness of the world. The gaze I search for must, instead of viewing nature as leading from an inseparable wholeness to a cataloged system, see it flow through that system back again into its original fullness. I have found such a gaze only once among my colleagues—namely, in Marjorie's eyes. I saw it there when, while we were out on our excursions, we realized that we could run headlong through the moss. Often, spellbound, I thought I saw this view in museums, as well: in paintings whose vision of nature overcame the merciless one-dimensionality of use-oriented observation, suggesting instead a mode of observing that aimed at identity between viewer and thing viewed.

Once I spoke with Mandelbaum about all this. He understood me well enough, but he warned me, saying, "Scientific observation is also an art, which needs to be learned. But if you *make* an art out of it, you will see without understanding. Consider Goethe, Ohlburg. He said, 'Because in knowledge as in reflection it is impossible to bring together a complete whole, because this part lacks the inner and that part lacks the outer, so must we think of science necessarily as an art, if we expect from it any sort of wholeness.' But be careful, Ohlburg. . . ."

At that time, at my graduation ceremony, when Mandelbaum, already somewhat in his cups, tried to get me to take these words to heart, I believed that I understood them. Now they do lie close to my heart. Now I understand them, because I have learned and suffered from their meaning. Mandelbaum himself no doubt suffered from doing science, but he wanted to cure this suffering through his own efforts. He sought the Archimedean point, where science coincides with knowledge. He will have found that point in the moss of the truth, in death. There, from out of the walled-off truth, from its joints and seams, knowledge proliferates.

STRANGE RELAPSE INTO THE SHADOWY REALM of terminology! Maidenhair moss stands out from all forest mosses by virtue of its impressive growth and its extraordinarily lush development. This voice that I listen for, this gaze that I miss, they flow from its thick cushions, from its smell when I crush it between my fingers, from its caress when I stretch my head toward it. The memory of what has happened to us, and the memory of what has not happened to us, conceals itself only to a limited extent in our brains. Our heads are walnuts, two twisted halves in a hard shell. But memories and knowledge reside in every part of our bodies. Because we no longer know how to remember with our brains, all the more do we lose the knowledge that we can remember with our bodies. So we know only that we know nothing—and barely that much.

Maidenhair moss, like all bryophytes, like all moss plants, is a key, a model, for finding our way back to remembrance, to full knowledge. For they are rootless. The most important task undertaken by the roots of other plants—namely, the absorption of water and of the nutrients that have accumulated within it—is achieved by the entire surface area of mosses. And only through water do the mosses propagate themselves. Thus, not only is the entire body of the moss a single sexual organ; what is more, all the moss's bodily functions have at their command a limitless capacity for memory. Propagation via water constitutes the moss's memory of its descent from algae, from the oceans of the Carboniferous period. And this memory will be triggered over and over again by water, but only by water.

The water of the stream is ice-cold. Our feet are red and swollen, blistered from our walk. We dangle them in the current.

Marjorie says, "If I were to let my feet swim away like fish, that would be a strange form of cell division."

"But I prefer other forms of reproduction."

"Yeah?"

"Yes."

"And which ones, for example?"

"If we lie down in the moss over there, I'll show you."

"But moss reproduces asexually."

"For sure. But it provides a comfortable basis for more highly developed systems. Don't you know that? And you a Scotswoman from the mossy Highlands?"

"No. I don't know."

The current pressed her foot against mine. Contact in swirling moisture. An autonomic impulse.

"My foot won't move," she says.

"I don't understand."

"My foos won't moos," she says to herself, under her breath.

"What are you saying?" I ask.

"It makes no sense," she says. "So that's why it makes sense." Now I understand, for it pulls us together into the symbiosis for which we have been waiting for weeks. We are mature; we go over to the moss. We lie in the moss, and it enfolds us. It grows together over us. It proliferates through us. We melt into it. It absorbs us. It divides us, then unites us again. It recedes; it penetrates. Sucks. Caresses. Blows. Cools. Warms. Under its yielding softness, the hardness of rock. It gives way. A falling. A floating. A short death. A reawakening. A free fall into contented happiness. A light sweat has fused us together, as though our bodies had produced a specific form of moss. The moss on the stones grows together with this body moss. It dries us. We dry together. We are, once again, two beings.

Drops on my face. Sweat. Or dew from the maidenhair moss in which I am lying. I don't know. I hear Mandelbaum's voice while

I watch the patches of sweat on Marjorie's blouse. Mandelbaum has stopped talking about the brown algae *Ectocarpus siliculosus*, venturing into topics that students in the seminar did not know whether to fall asleep over or be wide awake about.

"... life has varied the theme of combining two complementary cells with an imaginativeness that exceeds any—I repeat, *any*—attempt to conceptualize it, in its infinite scope."

Marjorie drops her eyes, smiling. Her patches of perspiration grow.

"If we follow the stream of life from its origins onward, the algae we already studied, and the mosses you know by now as well ..."

Our feet bump together.

"... the types of interconnection become ever more varied, ever richer, all the way up to the infinitely subtle strategies of the orchid, or even the highest heights of human

love . . . ah, well, yes. But the principle of
mutation brings an excess of uncertainty and
restlessness with it—in nature as in social
life. I don't refer to the pseudomutations of
the political brown algae, about which we
hear so much these days."

"Stay on topic, Mandelbaum!"

"Hear! Hear!"

The heckles are menacing. The brown
algae are propagating themselves. We stroll
through the English garden. Marjorie says,
"I don't think I'll stay in this country."

When she is mad, she speaks English;
when she is furious, she speaks Scottish.
Now she is speaking Scottish.

"These people sell the truth. I'm going
back. The Highlands are green. Munich
turns brown. Sorry, Lukas."

Marjorie went. She took her gaze with
her—and her parting tears.

The drops on my face. Sweat. Or dew

from the maidenhair moss. Whose tears? I listen for the voice; I search for the gaze. I saw it once more. She had given up her studies, gotten married, had three children. The gaze was still there. I traveled farther.

MY MOTHER WAS AFRAID OF SNAKES. On warm summer days, we went across the Hentings' pastures to the forest near Spohle. First went my father, swinging his walking stick with the coat of arms mounted on it, followed by Mother and flanked by us children. Following up in the rear was the housemaid with picnic basket, parasol, and blanket. We always chose the same clearing under a wide-crested oak; but before the blanket could be spread out over the herbs, grass, and mosses, my father would have to rummage around with his stick in order to scare away any potential snakes in the vicinity. Once a harmless, frightened blindworm had emerged from under the blanket and made off through the grass like lightning. It was not fast enough, however, to keep my mother from nearly fainting—though the hired girl, who herself had fallen into a hysterical though still relatively controlled shortness of breath, was just able to ward off my mother's fainting fit with the use of an eau de cologne–soaked handkerchief. The picnic was spoiled, however; even my father, who did not betray his feelings at the time, must have been deeply shocked, for he urged that we retreat immediately "for Mother's sake." Such consideration for "womanish moods" was normally not his style, but, as with moisture, all creeping things were scary to him.

Another time, the time that came to me through my fingertips just a short while ago, when I ran my hands through a thick cushion of maidenhair moss, my parents, the hired girl, and I were alone. Franz must have remained at home to study because of a bad mark at school. The snakes, in case there were any around on this August day, had been chased off, the food had been eaten, and my father was stretched out on the blanket, snoring with an open mouth. Mother sat next to him, browsing through a fashion magazine. The girl read a novel. I strolled through the feltlike underbrush that bordered our clearing. I went off the beaten path and came across a musty-smelling pond, in whose mud and thick weeds I searched for frogs. A branch lying under the surface of the water tripped me up. I fell lengthwise into the rotting, swampy morass. Soaked and stinking, I returned to the clearing. My mother was appalled; my father laughed briefly and then went back to sleep. It was some fifteen minutes by foot to the nearest quarry pond, so my mother sent the girl there to wash me and my clothes.

She took me by the hand and went with me toward the pond through the oppressive heat, which prefigured a thunderstorm.

"Take them off."

"But you have to look away."

She turned her back to me. I pulled off my things and jumped into the water, swimming far out. On the bank, the girl rinsed out my patched-up shirt and trousers.

"Come back! You need to wash yourself."

"Come and get me!"

"Come back here! I'll tell your parents!"

"You old tattletale! Come and get me!"

And then suddenly she really did remove her pale blue summer dress, climbed out of her underwear, jumped into the water, and swam out after me.

"Not so fast, Lukas. I can't swim very well."

I went slower, turned over on my back, played dead man, and faced the sun; but with unfamiliar curiosity, I sneaked a look at this body that, making its way through the water with clumsy motions, came toward me. She grabbed me by the leg.

"Finally—come along now."

"Pull me to shore."

"I can't do that."

"But it's really easy. Even Franz can do it. I'll make myself light for you."

She did not look at me; I did not look at her. I laid my hands on her shoulders, making myself light. Before my eyes, her reddish blond, flowing, dripping hair; under me, her legs spreading apart and closing rapidly. Her heavy breath.

"It's not going to work."

"Well then, I'll pull you."

I turned over on my back again, grabbed her under her armpits, felt her flinch, felt the base of her breasts, felt her back rise and fall in the water, felt her on my belly, felt myself stiffen, swam, grabbed her more firmly under her armpits, groaned, gasped, heard her breathe in fits and starts. When we had the ground under our feet, we continued to stand next to each other in the water. I began to wash myself.

"Do it right. You must rub."

"You do it."

"Turn around."

She waded toward me, rubbed my back with slow circular movements, scooped up water with her hands, and rubbed them over my hips and thighs.

"You have to do the front yourself."

"No, please—you do it."

I turned myself toward her; she had closed her eyes. She wiped my chest and my stomach, touched my childish hardness as if by accident, then gripped it firmly, pushed and rubbed, took my hand, guided it between her thighs, directed it with erratic motions through her reddish blond moss cushion. Characteristic of all Polytrichales, of Catherine's moss as well as maidenhair moss, is the underdeveloped stem, which spreads out when wet, creeping along the ground as though it were swimming. She breathed heavily. I didn't know what I felt. The upper twigs are, with the exception of their almost bare base, hairy with soft leaves. These widen out at the base to a sheath. On the tips of the foliated branches appear, in a reddish-colored felt protruding from the flower leaves, the plant's sexual organs.

Suddenly she pushed me away, jumping up onto the dry land. As she put on her clothes, the moss glowed.

"We have to get back. Come on."

She no longer took me by the hand. I was

twelve. We made our way back silently. The first heavy raindrops fell.

"Where were you, then?" my father wheezed out.

My mother said, "Now we're all going to get wet."

THE EVEN FLOW OF A SOFT, STEADY RAIN envelops everything in a gray-blue veil. The boundary between desiring and just letting things happen erodes more and more. The moss approaches me. In order to meet it, however ineffectually, I create the moisture that it needs to live. I walk around in the rain. In the rain, I place my ear on the earth and listen to the voice that is becoming louder. I look at the drops and they look back at me. Before I go to bed, I moisten my body. Sometimes I cry while dreaming. The fertilization of their egg cells can be completed only if mosses are adequately moisturized by dew or tears, flowing water or rain. My love is fulfilled. Sometimes in the rain I hear Mandelbaum's voice high above—and deep under—the brown algae, the mosses:

"Death is a part of love. As long as cells increase their number through cell division, their survival in a direct, uninterrupted lineage is ensured. But that line does not consist of unique individuals; when they die, they do not take any irreplaceable genetic traits with them. Rather, these traits remain preserved as clones in other cells, which all originate from the same far-distant ancestor. Love, however, means discontinuity between parents and their progeny. In this case, the descendants do not eliminate their forebears genetically, as with cell division, but only psychologically, through substitution and overcoming. To be sure, love always preserves the life of the parents, leaving something of them behind. But this something is eliminated very quickly by life.

"A wave, a rain shower, and it all passes away. It leaves behind no trace. What gets washed away, what death flushes away, are singular, unique creatures, which can never again be absolutely identically reproduced. What you are, Ohlburg, what I am, will never be again. Never. Death drowns forever the unique specimens that we are. That constitutes our uniqueness, because with algae death does not bring about an extinction of this sort. The only thing that survives us are our works, the children of our intellects, of what we know and feel. The river of death breaks over them, but they remain. They endure as a nonorganic, immaterial image of what we are. In them our essence continues to proliferate, mutating in the minds of those who come later. This happens until oblivion, that death at a distance, the only form of death worthy of the name—until oblivion, in all its dreadfulness, has penetrated the last dry place that remains."

SOMETHING IS STILL LEADING MY HAND and, through it, allowing the green signs to grow on the paper. The paper is very soft and porous, and the ink flows into it easily. It is as if I go along with it. In the process I feel myself becoming ever softer. A moist breath encircles me, soaks me through. I am cold.

MAY. A PECULIAR COLDNESS HAS ARRIVED. When I came here nine months ago, the lake was the lake, the forest the forest, and the moss moss, surrounded by strange words and names. When I began to lose myself in the moss, when I noticed that the moss even approached me and wanted me near, then the lake was no longer just a lake, the forest became more than a forest, and the moss became something other than moss.

Death is a rich green country, through which a moist wind blows. Deep in that country stands a thatched house. Perhaps it is half-decayed. Or burned down. The rain affects the flow of my thoughts and colors their greenness a watery blue. There are branches on the old trees up whose bark mosses climb. The wind makes the branches sound out, musical instruments of a universal murmuring. That is a depraved way of putting it, but I know it's true. Everything harmonizes here. Because this country is attuned to itself, it was able to have an influence on me. It allows things to resonate freely. What surrounds me is the original home of the mosses, a specific place that is nowhere. Mosses are, as is well known, no cosmopolitans. They are rooted rootlessly in particular locales.

I CAME HERE, AND NOW I am *in* the here. Now and forever. When I will have swum with the moss in the final country—swum to a place of eventful calm—the lake will again be the lake, the forest again be the forest, and the moss simply moss. And nothing else. I will be forest, lake, moss.

SOMETHING BECKONS. SOMETHING GROWS. Something proliferates. I follow passively, yet of my own free will. Everything is equally valid. I grow in all directions, am grown toward everywhere.

ONE WILL HAVE GOTTEN USED to considering death as the best thing that can happen to *Homo sapiens*. Plants always knew that and still know it better than we humans. There is an indefinable and, for that reason, true way of perceiving plants—a basic or primary awareness of individual plants as well as larger plant cultures. The dying out of a human being's animal life influences and stimulates this perceptual capacity enormously. What a person can learn if he or she becomes indifferent is immeasurable.

UNDER THE GHASTLY TERM *Leucobryum glaucum* the beauty of the white moss, the medal pillow, is brought under scientific control. I like to sleep on it. It serves as an indicator, as a pointer to soil that has been depleted, worn out through forestry. It as if the green and lovely plant is smiling out there, beckoning to me—as though it points beyond, floats ahead into a promising immensity. And, like so often, I strike out to follow it. It makes

me smile to think that wreath makers trans-
form it into grave decorations. The beckoning shows me the way to the gaze. I see now.

AT MATURITY, MOSS DOES NOT RELEASE its
spores immediately out of its capsules. They
become free-floating only when the surrounding tissue has finally rotted away. This
often takes up to a year, or longer.

THERE IS A SMALL FAMILY of turf-forming mosses
with only a single genus, *Splachnum*, which is
essentially restricted to Arctic areas. But for
a few days now it has flashed up around the
house; this in itself is amazing, given that the
heat and brightness are now constantly increasing. The luminous yellow- or red-colored
canopy of the moss is remarkably signal-like.
The facts of the matter are as follows.

With its flickering color and the indole-like smell that it exudes, this family of mosses, giving off an odor that is to me at once stimulating and narcotizing, now begins to settle in my beard, attracting insects that ensure the dissemination of its spores. This is quite exceptional for mosses. Even in the choice of its substrate, the home where it settles, this moss family demonstrates a special, worldly-wise cleverness. It grows exclusively on rotting organic matter. Of all the mosses, this moss is possibly the only one that will be able to rise up out of the evolutionary standstill into the colorful, fragrant realm of the higher plants. In the end, such presumptuousness, which I indulge negligently as the temperatures rise, is all for naught. But the glow, the swarming everywhere, the odor of deep blue—all this is a vehicle in which I can travel farther.

Translator's Note

I gratefully acknowledge the assistance I received from Nicola Bigwood's partial translation of *Moss*, submitted to fulfill the thesis requirement for her 2006 M.A. degree in Interpreting and Translating from the University of Bath. Bigwood's thesis constitutes an important resource for any reader of *Moss*, and though I did not discover the thesis until after completing a draft of my own translation, I drew on her work while making final revisions. I would also like to thank Klaus Modick and Elana Rosenthal for their invaluable feedback on previous drafts, and copyeditor Carol Edwards for her careful work at a later stage. All errors and infelicities, however, remain my own.